DOG MEN

Gavin Torvik

*Khalela,
Thank you for all the
support + enthusiasm.
It really means a lot.*

The following is based on a true story...

Published by Swann + Bedlam

Copyright © 2024 by Gavin Torvik

All rights reserved.

No part of this publication may be reproduced, distributed, or transmitted in any form or by any means, including photocopying, recording, or other electronic or mechanical methods, without the prior written permission of the publisher, except as permitted by U.S. copyright law. For permission requests, contact Swann + Bedlam.

The story, all names, characters, and incidents portrayed in this production are fictitious. No identification with actual persons (living or deceased), places, buildings, and products is intended or should be inferred.

Book Cover by The Parish Priest

Formatting by Swann + Bedlam
Editing by Swann + Bedlam
Logo by Rotten Fantom

Swann + Bedlam
an imprint of Punk AF Publishing
287 Exhibition St,
Melbourne, VIC 3000
Australia

swannbedlam.com

1st edition 2024

Leave A Review!!

By reading this book you are showing your support for indie authors and small presses like us. For this, we want to say thank you! If you would take a moment to leave a review whether it's on Amazon, Goodreads, or any other social media platform, we would very much appreciate it.

Books don't make themselves. Many countless hours go into creating the work you are about to read. Often times, indie authors you enjoy create these books as a result of raw passion, artistic expression, and pure drive, while also working day jobs. A review is a great tool to help get their books into as many hands as possible plus earn a piece of recognition for writers who truly deserve to have their names read and remembered.

At Swann + Bedlam we began publishing as a way to get wicked awesome books to readers like you. Our mission is to publish the offbeat, the macabre, the problem child, the outcast, and the flat-out weird. No genres, no boundaries, no agenda.

Once again thank you for reading and reviewing this work.

DON'T LET THE MAN BRING YOU DOWN.
Power to the people!

For Christopher.
Thank you for telling me.

At bottom, the emancipated are anarchists in the world of the "eternally feminine," the underprivileged whose most fundamental instinct is revenge.

-Friedrich Nietzsche

Ecce Homo

Part I

True Events

Chapter 1: Peanut Butter

Chris tore up the switchback. Logging trucks frequented these roads and if he met one there was nowhere to pull over, just a trench and a wall of trees on the uphill side, a precipice on the other. He hoped it was late enough in the day to avoid a head-on at the blind curves.

The '96 Tercel shrieked on right turns but took lefts with less protest. Its rust-pocked teal body was caked with dust. The driver-side window was stuck and the winder had detached, but he'd managed, by pressing his palm against the pane and pulling with nauseating friction, to crack it open a quarter inch at the top. He parked it for weeks at a time, so the airflow helped with the stale stink of cat piss that still lingered from the previous owner. It mixed with the smell of his spliffs and body odor into a potent stew.

But now his tires kicked up dust. He pulled over at one point to try to force the window shut but had been unable to budge it. Brown filth drifted in to grime up his face and made his nose and eyes run. There was nothing he could do but pull his scarf up over his mouth, squint, and wipe his watering eyes.

9

Chris had managed six weeks of winter at the only motel in New Denver, watching TV, reading, and out of sheer boredom, making two visits to the Japanese Internment Museum, the village's closest approximation of a tourist attraction. When he went broke, there was the free campground to the north of town, but they only let you stay for fourteen days. It wasn't patrolled much in the off-season, so he'd managed eighteen before the inevitable Conservation Officers arrived and made him pack up. It was okay; he knew places and knew how to find others.

He'd spent most of the last 4 weeks moving every few days, sometimes leaving the car to walk deeper into the woods, other times trekking back to the Tercel to drive off for Fletcher Creek or some other, more secret spot.

He ate peanut butter - on Dempster's flat bread at first and later off a spoon - and made oatmeal on his naphtha stove. Mornings he'd scoop Nabob coffee from a tub, brew it in his oatmeal pot, and pour it off the top, cowboy-style into his field mug. In the evenings, he'd steep rooibos tea and roast wieners that he forbade himself from eating during the day, a precious, juicy treat to look forward to.

When the weather was not ideal, he slept in the car. Mostly he slept in his nylon hammock or bivouacked on the ground. In the early days at the campground, he would wake up half-buried in fresh snow. By the time they kicked him out, it was becoming warmer. Now it was unseasonably hot despite the fact it was so early in the spring. It looked to be another summer of burning and smoke-clotted skies.

Chris had a sixteen-inch field knife - almost a machete, really - that was hefty enough to split firewood, and an ax for bigger jobs. He had a cellphone and a Bluetooth speaker, a battery pack to charge them. For a while, he had a fantasy novel, *Vazkor, Son of Vazkor*. He read it slowly over his time at the motel and twice in the days at the campground, then left it in the outhouse for someone else.

He still missed the outhouse, just as he missed the motel toilet, but he was no stranger to shitting outdoors.

He hadn't seen a familiar face in months, not since his grandma had kicked him out, so his chance meeting with Penny at the highway rest stop had been a ray of hope and a cause for excitement. The snow had retreated, except at the higher altitudes and the darkest depths of the forest. He felt a shift inside himself from the mode of pure survival that had dominated through the winter to a new hopefulness that bloomed with the spring buds.

If he was honest with himself (which he was), he was not sure Penny had liked him back in the day. Lots of people didn't. He had a tendency to wear out his welcome. To normal people, he was an alienating presence, too quiet, prone to making intense eye contact that was interpreted as aggression by men and women alike, though he meant to convey nonjudgmental interest and keen attention. Among weirdos, he was accused of being a bully, or a cop, or a misogynist, eventually and inevitably confronted by a delegated man or group of women and made unwelcome.

He was used to being quietly shunned or straight-up told to leave. Like at his grandma's or a friend's family home, numerous punk and noise houses, his job... he was less accustomed to being invited.

Chapter 2: Pull Out

Chris had been cruising north on BC-6 toward Highway 1 and decided to stop for a smoke at a pull-out viewpoint overlooking the valley.

It was early March but the sun beating through the dirty windows was intense, shining white-hot in a clear sky. The radio told Chris that wildfires already rampaged and conquered across the province but the smoke had not yet drifted here. He parked and cracked the door.

Dingdingding - he pulled the key to silence the open door alarm. He sat in the driver's seat for a moment and rolled a spliff, then came out and stepped over the concrete barricade, gazing out at the inverted hills reflected in the mercury surface of the lake.

A muffled thud of bass broke his solitude. The sub-bass rhythm announced the coming of a huge black pickup truck, a Dodge Ram 3500 extended cab sitting high on duallies. The windows were tinted so dark they matched the jet body. The EDM throb would have been ten years out of date anywhere else, the sort of West Coast bass music Chris would have spun at a beach party in 2010, but it was a perennial sound in the British Columbia interior.

The truck roared into the pull-out spewing diesel fumes. It parked a few spaces from the Tercel.

Three men emerged. They left the truck running. Chris was thankful to lose their voices to the truck's noise. He preferred the rumble of an engine, the rattling pound of the music to human conversation. The men passed a joint and looked out over the vista, talking.

Chris kept his distance, leaning against the safety barricade, the cliff at his toes, savoring the expanse and the tingling kiss of nicotine in his fingertips.

A man's voice rose over the noise, indistinct, buried in the ruckus but clear enough to draw Chris's attention. The trio was looking at him - or seemed to be - from behind their sunglasses.

Chris saw the raised chin and the open, miming mouth of the largest of the men. The speaker was tall, looked taller than Chris, thick of trunk and neck, in blue jeans, work boots, flannel, and denim jacket. He wore a close-cropped beard and battered baseball cap that shadowed his face. His companions were similarly dressed: jeans, cargo pants, a t-shirt here, a Fox Racing long sleeve there, one in a camouflage hat and mustache, on another a receding hairline trimmed to a buzz cut.

Chris tapped two fingers to his ear, shrugged, and turned back to the landscape. The roar of the engine cut to silence and the music stopped.

"Hell of a view, eh?"

Chris looked again. They were waiting for him to answer.

"Say again?"

"I said hell of a view."

"Hm," Chris replied. He nodded and turned once again to the panorama.

"You live around here?"

"Huh?"

The truck man let out a frustrated sigh and flicked his roach into the abyss beyond the barricade. His companions grinned and chuckled. The group moved a few steps closer.

"Where you from?"

"The coast."

This elicited a laugh.

"Which one?"

"Sorry, man, I'm not really into chatting right now. Just trying to get my eyes off the road, you know?"

The truck man stepped back theatrically, holding up his hands, palms outward. "My apologies. Didn't mean to burst your bubble, lone wolf."

The other two men smiled, enjoying the

15

show. Chris took a pull on his spliff.

"I appreciate the apology."

The Ram crew were returning to their vehicle but the man who spoke paused and turned to face Chris again.

"Just based on a feeling: you military?"

Chris considered whether to answer. After a time he said, "reserves. Gunner."

The truck man lingered, nodding. Through his aviator shades, he seemed to give an appraising look. Chris plucked a green leaf, folded the remnant of his spliff into it, snuffing it, and reached over the barricade to toss it in a nearby trash can.

A crescendo of burbling engine noise broke the silence. It was a half-ton, an old white Chevy covered in peeling flower decals and surf shop stickers. It rumbled into the pull-out and swung into a space on the passenger side of the Tercel.

The female driver shouted from her open window before she had even cut the engine.

"Oh my God, Chris?"

The big man in the baseball cap gave Chris a curt nod.

"Thank you for your service," he said and sauntered back to join his friends at the Ram.

The woman leapt down from the bench seat of her weather-worn Chevy. The door hung open,

16

the alarm *dinging* away.

Chris flung his arms to the sky like a referee calling good on a field goal.

"Penny!" he cried, stepping over the barricade and into the lot. "Great to see you! How long has it been?"

They embraced. Penny was always a committed hugger.

"How about finding you all the way out here," Chris said to the side of her blonde head.

"It's so wonderful to see you," she said into his shoulder. "What brings you back to the interior? I thought you were still on the Island. I'm not much for checking Facebook though." She pushed him back to arm's length and locked him in that warm brown-eyed gaze. "Oh my God, so many questions!"

"I've come inland," he said. "For the time being. Who knows. My contract ran up, and my landlord put the place up for sale and-" He shrugged and laughed.

"Alright! Free agent."

"Exactly. Free agent. So I'm just taking my time, camping out, roasting weenies. Got my hammock, got my tunes." He kicked the Tercel. "Got this little buddy here."

"Cute, cute."

"Couldn't handle being cooped up any more

17

anyway. Guess I just needed a little kick. What about you? You living out here?"

"Sort of. You could say that. Similar thing: for now. I'm actually up in Slave Lake, like, bought a house there, got a little garage studio, doing my market booth there these days."

"Oh, you're still doing the uh..." Chris snapped his fingers.

"Ceramics?" prompted Penny.

"Ceramics."

"Yeah, totally. That's most of my money these days. Though I'm still doing some, like, babysitting and stuff. Did a season of tree planting last year. But, yeah. Lately, though, you know, like the last year, I've been getting more into carving."

"Carving? That's awesome! Like wood?"

"Yep. Stone too."

"No way."

"Yeah. It doesn't sell like the pottery but it's just..." she flexed her fingers. "I dunno, I love it."

"You gotta have something that's just for you. It can't all be business. I mean, everybody's gotta have money but that can't be it."

"Exactly. Exactly. That's why I'm down here. Back in the old home turf, taking it easy, enjoying these views."

"Nothing like it, eh?"

18

"Amazing. I've got a canopy and folding tables so I've got, like, a portable outdoor studio. Just carving, feeling the air, hiking, driving around. Just feelin' this place."

"I love it. You carrying any with you? Carvings, I mean. I'd love to see your work."

"No, no, not right now anyway. Where are you staying?"

Chris shrugged. "Everywhere. Fletcher Creek, the hot springs. I've just been finding spots. I was heading for the provincial park but-"

"You'll never get a site. Not even overflow. You should come see where I'm at. So great. Nobody around, logging road access only, isolated. So beautiful. It's just on the other side of the lake. The sunset from there, oh my God. Breathtaking."

"That sounds great. Lead the way."

"Well, I'm running back into town right now. I have to help a friend with something. But I'll give you directions, it's easy. You can go and set up. I'll come meet you a little after dinner time. You'll know it when you see it, I've got a whole little workshop set up."

She gave directions. Not as simple as she had made it sound but Chris figured he had it down, he knew the area. When she left, he felt so good. It wasn't until later, when he was down the road

19

and out of sight of the pull out that he realized he didn't know if those men had left while
he talked to Penny or not. He wasn't sure why it
troubled him.

Chapter 3: Camp

The little four-door struggled up the private logging road in the fading light of a spring evening, creaking like it would snap in half, around blind curves and up steep rises, past yellow diamond signs warning of oncoming trucks. The headlights of the Tercel animated slats of shadow among the roadside trees.

Chris hunched over the wheel like an old woman, looking for the landmarks Penny had described and listening to the agonized protests of his poor Toyota. He thought he saw his turnoff: a blackened stump, the victim of some previous year's fires, like a crude rook, leaning over a pyramid of fist-size boulders about a foot high. He took the turn. The car rolled, hesitated, then struggled at the lip of the road before he floored it and pushed over onto a shady, rutted pathway.

A jouncing, clanking few minutes through a hall of tall conifers took him to a hillside clearcut and rimmed with evergreens. Gaps in the forest rim showed a new vantage on the lake.

The water caught fiery oranges from the setting sun. Ducks honked like car horns. The sun had fallen from view. The hills were great black mounds. He could tell stretches of highway by the brief streaks of headlights between the trees on the back lit hillside, fleeting as shooting stars.

He'd arrived: a yellow four-person tent, a fire pit Penny had built by arranging stones, a plastic camping chair, tracks where the Chevy had flattened the yellow grass, a canopy covering a jumble of carvings-in-progress on two plastic folding tables.

He popped the trunk, fetched his hammock and his cooler, and stood for a moment scooping peanut butter and licking it from a spoon.

The place had taken longer to find than Penny had said. She was running late, which tracked with what Chris knew of her.

Chapter 4: Weenie Roast

The woods were pitch black past the ring of firelight. Chris sat in Penny's rickety folding chair. It felt luxurious after weeks spent squatting like an ape. He hadn't sat in a chair since the motel.

His Bluetooth speaker murmured liquid drum 'n bass. With his field knife, he stripped a straightish branch into a crude little pike that he used to rotate an impaled wiener that blistered and spat hissing grease into the flames.

There was no phone service but that was common in this part of the Kootenays. At New Denver, only the landline in the motel office worked.

Earlier, he had walked the perimeter of the clearcut hunting for the perfect weenie stick. Then, toting his new spear, he had gone into Penny's canopied workshop, taking advantage of the remaining evening light to examine her pieces: animal heads so crudely hewn they were somewhere between childish and geometric abstraction, like artifacts of some lost primordial culture. Stones from thumb-size up to fist in the likeness of ducks, blade-beaked raptors, and puggish dog heads lay on the tables like relics from an archaeological dig waiting to be sorted. Willy-nilly among the stones were mallets and chisels, large nails, bent screwdrivers, and knives in an array of sizes.

Strewn about the ground and propped against table legs was a motley assortment of masks carved of wood or thick sheaths of bark. Some mimicked the primitive animism of the stones, others seemed more intuitively carved. Penny's gouges and holes followed the asymmetric, organic contours of the wood. Crooked mouths grinned and gaped and gave weird ambivalent expressions that he didn't know how to read. Eye holes were placed where once-living wood dictated, often heavily skewed such that both could not be looked through at the same time. They intrigued him. Chris looked forward to talking to her about them - assuming she hadn't flaked.

As he turned his wiener over the flames, the orange firelight flirted with the night under the canopy, catching the grooves and contours of the heads, mutating their expressions from one moment to the next. The animated menagerie was like a mute choir singing a dissonant hymn lost to human memory.

***

White light slashed through the trees in vertical razorblade beams like the coming of a UFO. The white swords resolved into circular sprays from twin white suns. A truck by the sound and size, though Chris could not yet see with any certainty. Just engine sound, light, and a growing, rhythmic pulse of bass.

As the vehicle pulled in he could see this was not Penny's flowery old long box but a shining, night-black Ram, its interior cloaked by illegal tint that matched the body. Dubstep thrummed behind the engine growl. It crunched its way into the clearing to stop just inside Chris's glowing ring.

Chris shaded his eyes against the halogens. The front passenger side window whirred smoothly down and the music blared louder, shouting out the opening like the window was the mouth and the music the voice of the great vehicle. A black tongue curled out from that mouth: a man cast into spectral relief, almost lost behind the light. He shouted over the noise.

"You Chris?"

"Who're you?"

"Your name's Chris, right?"

Chris set his meat aside, propping the stick carefully against the arm of his chair. He rose from his seat and walked around the fire pit,

25

squinting and shading his face against the glare. The protruding man cut a skeletal figure.

"What's up," said Chris.

"Your friend. The chick you were talkin' to at the pull out. Heard you talkin' 'bout this place and thought we'd come check it out. Sounded nice. So we're comin' up the road and seen your girl. She got'n an accident. Off the shoulder right into a tree. Lucky we were comin' along. We got her here, we gotta take her into Nelson, man."

"Penny?"

"We wanted to take her right to the hospital but she kept sayin' how you'd be out here waiting for her. Worried and all that. So we came for you. She hit her head."

Chris tried angles of vantage, struggling to see into the dark interior. From where he was he could make out nothing, the lights were too bright. Stepping to the passenger side, out of the direct beam, he saw only more blackness and a faint blue glow from the stereo console. But he could see the skeleton more clearly. It was not the man he had spoken to at the rest stop but one of his buddies, the one with the mustache and camo hat. Out of the sun, he had ditched his wraparound Oakleys in favor of rectangular eyeglasses.

Mustache Man kept talking. "Pretty sure she

has a concussion, man, you-"

Chris cut him off, raising his voice: "Pen, you alright?"

He thought he heard something but he wasn't sure. The man leaning out never took his eyes off Chris.

"Hey, could you guys cut the beats?" Chris said.

The volume decreased a little.

"Penny?"

The reply that came was a small, barely audible "yeah?"

Chris moved in closer, hoping to adjust his pupils to the blackness inside.

The feminine voice came again: "I'm here."

Chris stepped within arm's reach of the Mustache Man and, even though he was six-two, lifted himself on tiptoe to see inside. The rear passenger window of the extended cab was shut tight, and the man with the mustache blocked most of his view through the front.

He walked the length of the truck, almost blind, red blotches clouding his vision. When he got to the end of the box, the tail lights aided him with their red burn. He put a hand on the fender to guide himself and stepped carefully on the rooty ground. He breathed diesel stink.

At the rear driver-side door, away from the

stare of the Mustache Man, Chris hopped up onto the runner board and pressed his face to the dark glass.

The power window to his left came down with a buzz like a swarm of flies. The driver was the large man who had spoken at the pull-out. Without sunglasses, his eyes were beady and sunken, too close together for the massive head. The tail lights set the Cro-magnon brow and cheeks aglow while setting the eye sockets in shadow. Despite his inelegant proportions, there was something clever in his face, a remote and calculating contempt that Chris had detected at the viewpoint. Something in the set of the jaw, the posture, the tone of voice...

"You gonna climb all over my truck or you gonna get in?"

Chris said nothing.

"Or you wanna ride all the way clinging to the side like that? It's a bumpy road."

Chris hopped off the runner, backed away, then walked back to his chair. He sat and took up his wiener stick, hovering it once again over the flames. He kept his eyes on the sausage, turning it with meticulous steadiness, making a show of his focus.

He heard muffled voices over the din of music. Then the music pounded louder. The truck lunged toward him with a snarl and a reek of diesel, swung sideways, swooped into a three-point turn, and almost backed into the tent.

The ass of the truck faced Chris, the muffler belching. The brake lights bathed his face with red.

The Truck Driver looked back at him.

"This is a nice place," he hollered. "Maybe after we drop your friend off we'll come back."

Chris was silent, watching his wiener. The Ram chugged out of the clearing and onto the trail. He watched the tail lights shrink in the darkness like red eyes staring him down.

Chapter 5: Roll Over

They brought dogs.

Chris knew they'd be back, so he had avoided the tent and instead set up his hammock some meters away under the heavy shadow of twin firs at the edge of the clearing. They must have parked downhill and walked in.

A breeze had picked up as the night deepened and he wasn't sure if he'd hear them over the whispering treetops. But three men in boots were easy enough to pick out in the end. It took Chris a moment to notice the dogs. He could not at first pick out the swish and patter of the canines. It was only when one of them passed a gap in the trees and cast a silhouette that Chris realized what was really going on. After that, he could make out the hot animal panting. He could tell their direction and was even able to see them once they entered the clearing, shadows on shadows, whispering hushed commands to their dogs in the blue-black night.

Chris refused, on principle, to wait up all night crouched and alert. Earlier, he had climbed into his hammock hoping to sleep, hoping he would wake in the morning alone and prove a point to himself. Now he was hung between trunks, twenty meters from the camp, swinging in the breeze at the edge of the clear-cut, thinking about how to reach ground without detection.

He lifted a leg over the edge of the hammock and rolled his shoulders after it, tilting the hammock and feeling for the forest floor with a foot. He leaned away from the clearing into the dark of the surrounding firs. He had propped his ax against the trunk nearest to his head. Chris reached for it, putting some of his weight against it like a cane so he wouldn't tip over and spill out.

The shadow-shapes approached the Tercel. A flashlight clicked on and the beam scanned around the interior of the car, casting its peripheral glow on the faces of the men, imbuing them with a ghoulish radiance. The flashlight clicked off. The group moved to the tent and arranged themselves on three sides. Two lights clicked on, setting the reflective webbing of the rainfly aglow.

"Come out of the tent."

Chris skirted the edge of the campsite in a commando hunch until he had a direct line to the driver's side of the Tercel. This maneuver put him a little behind the trio on their flank. His heart pounded. He hoped the dogs would not be-

31

tray him.

The animals shifted and paced but hung close to their masters.

"Chris. Wake up. Come out."

A sick fear rose in him. He thought of bolting, scurrying down the mountainside, and following the lake shore to the highway in hopes of hitching a ride. Nearly all his possessions were in the Tercel save the hammock, the ax in his hands, the blade at his waist, and the useless phone in the pocket of his cargo pants. It would be bad enough to abandon the hammock. Losing the car was unthinkable. The thought of trying to hitchhike with a machete and an ax was laughable but he could just ditch them too...

The last time he'd tried to hitchhike, no one had stopped for him except the cops.

Chris couldn't see much. Panic pressed on his brain and tightened his chest, threatening to destabilize him. He could have sworn one of the dogs cocked a head in his direction. He took deep and steady breaths.

As a boy, he had been a passenger in a stolen car. When the police pulled them over, everyone inside ran. Chris hid under a parked van but the cops had dogs and one of the dogs found him. It tore a hunk of flesh from his right arm at the inside of the elbow while dragging him out.

He had felt then, in his child's mind, that they weren't supposed to do that. He thought that they were supposed to corner you and bark until the officers came to put the cuffs on. The dog had ripped out a chunk of muscle and mangled nerves. The hand was never the same. He was lucky to be left-handed.

So Chris threw the ax.

It spun end over end and clipped one of the men above the ear with a hollow, moist *boonk* that startled the others. The flashlight fell to the dry grass, the beam cast askew. The struck man lifted a hand to his temple and stood for a second, frozen.

"The fuck...?"

He swayed, staggered, and collapsed.

Chris had already sprinted most of the way to the car, stealth abandoned. Almost there.

"Shit! Get 'im, get 'im!"

Wet barks from the dogs, the pounding of their little feet. They were closing on him fast, charging in to take him from the side.

The Tercel door squeaked open. Chris was in. The keys waited for him in the ignition block.

Dingdingdingding - he slammed the door and cranked it. The engine wheezed to life. For some reason, he worried that he would back over one of the dogs. For some reason, it would be

33

unbearable to do so.

Chris hit reverse, whipped ninety degrees, and shifted to first. The tires spun, got a grip, and he finally swerved out toward the trail.

In his memory, Chris felt his 2004 Camry splitting at the front axle and collapsing as he pulled out of a parking space in Victoria years prior. But the Tercel held together. It screamed but it held.

Chris convulsed at the impact of some hefty projectile against the rear window. He ducked his head but that was it. He was away. Into the twin ruts and out. He hoped they had parked on the road below and not blocked the trail.

The Toyota clattered and creaked. The suspension whined. The frame rattled. The seat vibrated beneath him. The check engine light glowed orange and a diminutive alarm rang out its dainty dismay. His headlights scarcely illuminated more than a few meters of trail in the reckless jouncing, shining now on the trees, now on a rise in the terrain ahead, now reflecting off a sign: PRIVATE PROPERTY. And another: WATCH FOR TRUCKS.

Chris made the end of the line, rocked up over the spine that separated the narrow trail from the gravel road, and cranked a sharp left, fishtailing down toward Highway 6.

A creature, brown, on four legs, leaped from the right-hand roadside. In the split second it was visible it seemed less like the animal reflected his headlights and more like it gave off its own ghostly phosphorescence, a brown murk shot through with streaks of platinum radiance.

But this was no ghost; it was solid. It thunked against his right headlight and went under the tire, rattling the bones of the Tercel. Chris felt the chassis snap as if it were his own femur. His throat plummeted to his guts at the thought that he had hit one of the dogs after all. The vehicle lurched hard. He slammed the brake and tried to correct but it didn't matter. There wasn't enough road. He went over and the hillside sucked him down.

The vehicle plummeted, collided with a tree trunk, and crumpled. The car had no airbag. His face hit the steering wheel and the world turned over.

Chapter 6: Machine Dream I (Tercel)

Motors rumbled. Chris was surrounded, ringed in by vehicles that coughed foul smoke. Yellow headlights came from every direction, blinding him. Tinnitus rang in his ears.

He was naked, scrambling on his belly across loose brown dust. The lamps cast long shadows that blurred and canceled each other in intersecting trajectories of light.

Around him, a dizzying array of images: screaming, jeering men's faces; hooting, hollering mouths ringed by wiry facial hair and sandpaper stubble, filled with crooked teeth, yellow as the vehicle lights, set like horrible gems in receding, discolored gums; men's bodies, shifting, smoky ghost-men only semi-visible in the glare, in bluejeans, chests bare, hair prickling and curling from lumpy torsos; boots in dirt, ratty sneakers scraping, jostling, kicking up dust that sparkled in the air; dogs barking and pulling at leads and chokers, a terrible cacophony of men and animals and clattering chains; the smell of diesel and dust...

Chris knew the dog was on him, a German Shepherd. He knew it bore down on him, snarling with a wet mouth, though he dared not look back. He crawled for the cover of a parked car, a Toyota Tercel that shone with glossy new teal paint.

Someone else was there but he couldn't see. He didn't know who it was but it was there.

His belly was raw, irritated by the fine dirt beneath him. He was almost under the car but the dog was on him. The men roared. He groped in the dust and felt a stone the size of one hemisphere of a brain meet his palm. He seized it.

The dog overtook him. Its jaw locked on his arm and it dragged him around in a crescent. The flesh of the arm split and the animal tore a long strip of skin and muscle, peeling his forearm like a banana. It didn't hurt, it just felt cold.

Chris struck at it with the rock, bringing his bludgeon down on the animal's skull with a sickening crack. It whimpered.

Gripped with disgust and shame at what he had done, Chris tossed the rock aside but the dog had no such mercy. The hairy ghosts that ringed him hooted with laughter. The dog recovered and snarled, warm drool dripping onto him as it lunged for a second attack. Chris got hold of a forepaw and bit down but his teeth broke against the bone, cracking first in vertical hairline fractures and then crumbling like dirt clumps.

The dog seized Chris by the back of the neck and the rubble of his teeth spilled from his mouth. The animal was bigger than he had imagined. It shook him like a rabbit. He could feel his brain shaking in his head, scrambling, everything went gray. White flakes of tooth fell with spittle that rained from his mouth.

The dog's jaws came loose and he was sailing across the dirt. His vision was clouded by motion blur, the faces blending together into a great tumorous mass of savage men and dogs.

Chris rose to his knees. The dog mounted him from behind, pushing him down, and clamped on with teeth that dug into his scalp. Chris pushed himself backward and fell upon it, twisted, and rolled away.

The dog seized his arm once again, clamped like a bear trap, snarling. Chris took up the rock and brought it down, the impact jarring through the creature's skull causing it to press its teeth deeper into the wound, hammering fangs into his arm like nails. The skull shattered. The mouth grip slackened. Chris pried the jaws off his arm and shoved the animal away.

He tried to stand, got only part way, and collapsed. Chris pushed himself up on his knees like a penitent and brought the rock down dealing blow after blow, pulping the skull. Brains poured from the wrecked head.

Chris knelt in the dust, panting in the filthy air. He smelled woodsmoke and vehicle exhaust. The dogs from the periphery were set loose, shepherds and rottweilers and pit bulls, retrievers and collies, and stout terriers. The pack sniffed around him, pacing a wide circle, then closed in and began to eat the brains that spilled from the head Chris had crushed. They nuzzled in, devouring one of their own, docile, happy. Tails wagged. The men were gone.

Overcome with rage, terror, shame, and disgust, Chris opened his mouth to scream, but the only sound that came was a delicate electronic *dingdingdingding...*

***

Chris was slumped against the steering wheel. Hiss of escaping steam and coolant, pops of cooling metal, that incessant little alarm. The Tercel wanted service.

It was day but the light was odd. Sterile, uniform. Hospital light. He couldn't pinpoint the direction of the sun and he felt no warmth.

He raised his head. A huge gray wolf stood on the smashed hood of the Tercel. The tree he hit loomed behind it.

The wolf did not look at him but gazed over the top of the car. Chris wanted to turn, to look back and see what it saw. He managed a partial turn to the left where the door hung open and the side mirror swung on tendons of wire, reflecting only the teal of the door panel. He twisted - an agony to his neck - and managed a peripheral peek over his shoulder.

He saw a man. No, a figure. Man-like, but indistinct somehow. A man shape but the proportions were all wrong.

Chris said, "Please help me."

The grotesque figure said nothing. Maybe it couldn't hear him.

Chris turned back to the front of the vehicle, his neck cracking severely. The wolf was gone. The weird figure stood just past the crumpled hood, where the tree should have been. Though Chris looked at it dead on, he could not see it much clearer, as if he were still looking through peripheral vision. The body was squat, clad in rough pale brown robes like burlap. The head was much too large, like an apple but lumpier, misshapen, almost comical, the proportions of a bobble head, the flesh the color of a bruise.

He felt wetness on his right arm. A German Shepherd lay in the passenger seat, lapping at blood that poured from a wound in the crook of his elbow. Chris felt an imminent, anxious pressure as if at any moment it might clamp onto him like a trap.

The Bobblehead made a sign with its left hand, raising its index finger and pinky straight up like devil horns, and pursing the tips of the middle finger, ring finger, and thumb into a long pointed snout, the final effect like a gang sign version of the head of Anubis.

Behind the being, a hideous red fractal burning, glowing, unfolding. White noise and rattling, building, building, building, like the whole universe was convulsing, the blurred man-thing becoming a brown smear against the swirling gore. It opened its hands. More swirling fractals spewed forth, red, yellow, black, and brown-mottled pink, ribbed like the roof of a dog's mouth, unfurling and engulfing the air, enclosing him, overtaking everything, swamping his vision. The wash of fleshy fractals caressed his face, moist and firm.

Chris heard words like dribbles:

"Good boy."

Chapter 7: In and Out

Fuckin' moron.

Ain't too stupid, he got the drop on us.

I love a fight man, I like it when they got somethin' in 'em.

Reggie's gonna be fucked though.

He's a fuckin' faggot-ass anyway.

How's he doing?

Coming and going.

Should we give 'im something? He's lookin' pretty rough.

Nah. C'mon help me lift him out.

If his spine is broken we'll kill him.

Fuck it.

Dingdingdingdingding

ding ding ding

ding ding

ding

ding

ding

ding

Red fractals of dog mouths bloomed in the darkness like smoke.

***

"Don't worry, we gotcha, bud."

The voice of the Truck Driver.

Hands on him. Pain. Shifting light and cool air. A wash of white so bright it felt like it seared him. He got glimpses: swimming faces, twisted, torn metal, a shining black obelisk, an endless abyss of light and darkness. Reality blurred and blanked like a computer glitch.

Now he saw the sky. Void punctuated by pinpoints of starlight. The deeper shadows of swaying tree limbs, the lives of the forest looking down at him and dancing their unknowable rite. The foliage whispered secrets he could almost understand.

Part II

Raw Dog

Chapter 8: Wet

"Wake up, faggot."

Chris exploded into consciousness with a convulsion like an electric shock. His mind was in shards. He felt as if his head had burst like a water balloon, soaking him with gore so cold it burned. His whole body was pulsing in agony. The earth spun too fast, drifting blotches in his eyes like filthy dishwater spiraling down a drain.

A man-shape swam into focus, leaning at a ninety-degree angle. Chris took a moment to re-orient himself and realized it was the Mustache Man towering over him, holding a plastic bucket. He wore a tactical belt at his waist hung with pouches, a holster where the butt of a taser stuck out, and a straight black truncheon dangling almost to his knee.

Face down and naked on frigid concrete, Chris was soaked. Water ran in gray rivulets to be slurped up by a gurgling floor drain. His face felt tender pressed against the hard surface. His chest ached, sending stabbing pains through his torso that made him stop short when inhaling. He blinked slowly. When he reached gingerly to touch his aching body, he found first that his wrists were locked together, and second, that the upper half of his torso was wrapped snug in tensor bandages. He felt mummified.

"Get up."

Chris tried to push himself to all fours but his arms felt like jelly and his wrists burned with pain. His limbs shook. He tried to spread his knees out to steady himself and found his ankles bound together with a thin cord that dug into his flesh, probably a zap strap. He lost balance and collapsed, smacking his tender face to the concrete.

Mustache Man laughed.

Chris felt a constriction in his throat, a tightness of thirst and apprehension. His voice was a weak croak, barely more than a whisper. "What the fuck man..."

One of the booted feet shot out to slam him in the kidney. "Shut up," said the Mustache Man, contempt saturating every word.

"Man, what the fuck-"

The second kick set Chris to coughing and gagging. As he sputtered, the bucket came down on him again and again, raining with an unsteady rhythm of resonating sounds like a hollow drum.

"Shut! The! Fuck! Up!"

There followed a scraping sound paired with a squeaking of hinges. A rhombus of dirty light

47

fell across Chris's face. Next came the heavy clomp of boot falls and the voice of the Truck Driver.

"Easy. Don't hurt him any worse." The Truck Driver didn't sound troubled, only gently amused.

"What's it matter? I'm puttin' money against this faggot."

"Shut up," said the Driver. He stepped over Chris and squatted into his line of vision. Locked with those sunken brown eyes, ringed with purple, Chris felt a cold and desperate rage come over him.

"Man, fuck this," choked Chris. "Fuck you."

"You don't say a word. Ever," said the Truck Driver, his voice quiet and level. "Or I let him-" he nodded toward the Mustache Man - "do whatever he wants to you."

"What, fuck my ass?" Chris tried to look up at the Mustache Man's face but he couldn't quite get up to eye level. He spoke to the man's denim groin, where the bucket handle dangled in a slack hand. His mouth tasted of iron and bile. "Try it, homo."

The Driver chuckled. "You didn't have much to say back at your campsite. What changed?"

Chris hocked a thick wad of phlegm onto the floor by the Driver's steel-shod toes. "Speak-

48

ing of which: how's your buddy?" Chris inquired. "Tell him I'm sorry. The ax just slipped."

The Driver smiled.

"I'm clumsy," said Chris.

"Get up."

"You know I can't."

The Truck Driver rose and stepped back. Mustache Man charged in, kicking Chris in the side of the ribs. Chris tried to roll away but the move only exposed his gut. Two rapid blows to the stomach and Chris folded vomiting yellow bile that ran down his chin and pooled on the concrete next to his head. His chest was an inferno. He curled into a protective fetal position, dragging vomit with his face. The Mustache Man kicked his shins, his face, his guarding forearms, then stepped over Chris and began beating him in the lower back, ass, and thighs.

"That's enough," said the Driver. Two pairs of hands seized Chris under the armpits and hauled him to his feet. A white bolt of pain blasted through him from crown to ankles. His right knee, hips, and ribs ached horribly, his right arm tingled with numbness in a way he hadn't felt in thirty years. Every breath hurt.

They dragged him, his feet following like a fishtail, to a corner of the room, hoisted him higher so his feet were under him, and let go. He

49

crumpled immediately.

"Fuckin' pathetic," sighed the Mustache Man.

"Look here," the Truck Driver said.

Chris stared at the wall. He worried about another beating. In his present condition, he worried he wouldn't be able to stand it, that they would beat him to death. But he didn't look up, he looked at the wall and was silent.

"Alright then," said the Truck Driver. "You'll learn eventually."

Chris jumped at the impact of a white plastic bucket that dropped to the floor in his line of sight.

"You shit in this. Piss in the floor drain," said the Driver. "You shit on the floor and you eat it."

The two captors walked for the door.

"This is the gayest shit ever," Chris said as loud as he could manage, still staring at the wall.

There was no response. Just departing footfalls, the scrape of the door, and the click of a lock.

50

Chapter 9: Hot Car

They put a sack on his head and dragged him out by the armpits. The basement air outside his fetid room smelled wet and felt cool.

A routine had set in. Chris had a rough estimate of how long he had been there, based on how often they brought him food and water.

How often he would squat over his bucket to shit.

How often the Mustache Man came in with a look of absolute hatred to take the bucket, carry it at arm's length down the hall, returning some time later with a more or less rinsed but still stinking pail.

Twice they had come in for no reason other than to spray him with a hose fitted with a high-pressure nozzle. Some combination of torment and hygiene, Chris figured.

The more time passed, the harder it was to be sure of his accuracy. He guessed six weeks, maybe two months. So it was either mid-spring or heading into summer. But what is the margin of error when you have no window, spend ninety percent of your time in absolute darkness, and judge the calendar by the fact that you've shit two dozen times?

Chris heard the men carrying him huff, felt himself hoisted, and his ankles bumped against a wooden ledge, then another, then another. He was being dragged up a flight of raw wooden stairs that chafed against his feet and caught at the zap straps on his ankles. Light shone against the fabric of the hood he wore and he could almost see between the fibers, though even that light stung his eyes. The air coming down now was hot and smelled of woodsmoke.

Chris heard their panting, felt the jerkiness with which they hauled, and took pleasure in being uncooperative, passive, dead weight. Let them struggle with him. They hadn't been feeding him well, but they also hadn't kept him long enough for significant weight loss. He had gone in at almost two hundred pounds, with a powerful physique built by hauling his gear for miles.

Even when Chris had been at his most down in the dumps, he had taken satisfaction from multi-day hikes, following some stream or river, or making for the peak of a mountain, just for the pleasure of it. He was hard and heavy and knew he was not easy cargo. This gave him as much pleasure as was available, under the circumstances. He smiled under his hood.

Beneath the smoke, he smelled dust and dry grass. It was likely still springtime, and if so, it was unseasonably hot and sure to be a dire summer.

The men dropped Chris in the grass, which was dry as hay and scratched his skin. He sneezed, sending a shock through his ribs and curling him into an involuntary ball.

The hood was yanked from his head and he blinked into painful brightness. As he adjusted, he looked toward the treetops. The sky was almost blue, the sun discolored by a faint gray-white haze but still beating down with merciless intensity, unbroken by clouds.

He heard the thick click of a car door opening. The two men gripped him once more under the armpits. Chris saw a defunct patrol car, an old Ford Crown Vic Police Interceptor, the insignia sun-bleached and peeling, its naked rims up on cinder blocks. He squinted against the glare of sunlight on white paint.

They pushed him through the open door, shoved him along the hard bench seat, and locked him inside.

The air was thick and stale. It smelled of rotting upholstery, hot vinyl, and dust.

Chris lay there a while, catching his breath, letting his ribs ease from the pain of the sneeze and the man-handling. He blinked, letting his dungeon-trained eyes grow accustomed to the natural light. Silence pressed inside his ears like cotton wads. It was hard to breathe fully, the air was stifling.

Already, sweat was beginning to bead on his brow, his armpits, and the small of his back. The tattered vinyl of the bench burned his skin where it pressed upon his bare ass, thighs, and shoulder blades. Chris peeled himself up with a sound like tearing Velcro.

His brains lurched in his skull as he sat up fully. He tugged at the cage that bisected the vehicle. It rattled, but he found it more solid than he had thought.

Looking outside, his jailers watched him with faces as blank as Easter Island heads. Mustache Man pulled on a cigarette.

Chris laid back on the bench and kicked out at the window with his bound feet. The impact sent a burst of tingling pain through his swollen soles. It reverberated along his shins to his knees. He kicked again. A dull thud. The window did not budge. He tried once more. He felt like his shins would splinter like kindling before the glass gave way.

The pain and futility enraged him. Chris clenched his jaw and struck out over and over, pounding the window as fast as he could tuck his knees up to his chest and piston his legs out

54

until his chest burned, sweat stung his eyes, and he realized how dizzy he had made himself.

Chris dropped his head to the bench, his legs propped up on the window sill, and fought the urge to throw up. He was too tall to lay out fully on the bench, so he rolled to his side and tucked his legs up, his mouth slimed with a film of dehydration.

The blur of the sun beat down through the haze. He tried to think. He was outside, it seemed like an opportunity. If he could get out, maybe he could do something, find some heavy object amid the detritus nearby, club them with it, cut his bonds, and run. If he were to do anything, he'd have to do it soon before the heat and the stale air and the dehydration incapacitated him.

In the basement, he'd had no means to track time but the loose guesses guided by his feedings and bowel movements. Now, he reasoned, it was early in the day. Late morning or early afternoon at the latest. If the men meant to fry him in the car they would probably keep him there for hours, through the heat of the day.

He wondered, not for the first time, why? Were they weakening him to rape him? To allow others to rape him? Was it pure sadism? Had he done something to offend them? Were they acting on behalf of someone who felt he had wronged them?

Finding the bench seat unbearable, he crawled down to the floor and nestled against the front of the seat, trying to press himself into the meager semi-shade in the crook between the bench and the floor. He could only get his back in there, most of his nakedness roasting in the dusty air.

He tried to breathe with discipline, to suck in air slowly and deeply, imagining himself in a sauna or steam room. It was Toonie Tuesday at the community center. He tried to think of anything but his dry, sour mouth, tried to do anything but fantasize about water. He knew that doing so was a trap that would drive him mad.

***

Finally, they pulled him out by the legs. By that point he was semi-conscious. He wasn't sure if he had passed out fully or was just in a daze. The back of his head struck packed earth. The air was divinely cool, the sun behind the treetops. He writhed and blinked in a feverish delirium.

Someone kicked him.

"Up."

He squirmed on the ground like a worm. They gripped him by the triceps and scooped him up, grunting as they did so. Their hands were cool and clammy. His head lolled and his cheek scraped against the sandpaper stubble of the Mustache Man's cheek. He felt a huff of breath on his face, smelling alcohol from the mouth and tobacco in the hair as the Mustache Man grunted his exertion.

Chris was seized by a full-body heave. His head jerked forward and he spewed a yellow syrup that swung from his nostrils and chin in stinking, acidic spiderwebs, dribbling down to entangle itself in the hair on his stomach and crotch.

Mustache Man abruptly let go, the Truck Driver holding only a half-second longer, so that as Chris fell, he spun, landing hard on his right shoulder. Dust and plant matter burst from the desiccated earth and no sooner had he impacted than Mustache Man seized him by the hair and ground his face into the spot where a few strings of yellow slop had fallen.

"You almost puked on my fucking boots, you filthy animal."

"A'right, a'right," came the voice of the Driver from above. He bent and with a tug and a snap, Chris felt the strap about his ankles cut free.

"Help me get him back up."

They pulled their prisoner upright once again. Chris's head lolled and he wanted to kick them, to strike out, but found he could barely lift his feet. He made a feeble attempt to trip up the Mustache Man, to no effect. The Driver laughed. "Still got some fight in ya, eh?"

They let him go again and Chris rag-dolled and hit the ground. The Driver laughed and the Mustache Man groaned with disgust.

Back up again.

"You walk or you go back in the car."

Vision lurched. All he could see, his head hanging, were boots and his own bare feet, caked with dust from the earth and dried blood from where the ties had rubbed his ankles raw. The friction wounds made multicolored rings: shredded and red in the center, then purple, green, and finally a yellow that tapered into the tone of his skin.

He raised his head and turned to look the Truck Driver in the eye. Those sunken, beady eyes stared back, steady as ever. Mustache Man shoved the hood over his head and everything went dark again.

"Walk."

Chris jerked his arms away and took a step.

"Atta boy."

58

From that point on they would steady him periodically when he threatened to tumble to one side or the other. More than once he tripped on some uneven terrain or an object and hit the ground hard.

He yearned for the soothing cool of the basement. The nausea would pass. They'd have to give him water eventually. Without the ankle bracelet, maybe his legs would heal and he would grow strong again.

Chapter 10: Run

Chris marched. After a time, the swish of grass under his feet became the scrape of gravel. Rocks dug into his soles.

The hood came off, revealing the gray glow of the sky and a driveway that snaked off to vanish into the surrounding trees. They were in another part of the property. Chris looked over his shoulder and saw the house behind him, a split-level structure with weather-worn metal slats of siding and a flat patio atop a two-bay garage. Nearby a half-dozen vehicles in varying states of repair clustered on the driveway - trucks, cars, a van, and mixed among them, a cattle trailer and several flatbed and box trailers.

The sun was well behind the tree line now and the coolness of the air brought Chris some relief, though not much, given his mouth was still glued with thirst, his veins bulged, and his sides hurt.

A truck was parked directly behind him. Not the Ram but a huge old F-250 raised so high Chris could make eye contact with the headlights. His wardens left him there swaying on his feet and climbed into the cab.

The engine roared to life, a loose, percussive knocking. The headlights flashed on and the truck lurched forward. Chris fell.

"You lay in the road," shouted the driver over the bass gurgle of the Ford, "and I'll run you over. Get up!"

Chris clambered to his feet. His palms and knees were bloodied by the pebbles. The raw flesh where the straps had dug in around his ankles itched with embedded grit.

The truck lunged forward again and this time it kept coming. Chris stumbled again. He threw out his arms to catch himself, abrading his hands further on the rough terrain. He loped forward in a bear crawl, then rose without ease to his feet.

The lifted truck came on at idling speed, pressing in closer and closer. He could smell the hot metal, the stink of grease, and diesel fumes mingling with the woodsmoke in the air. He felt the engine heat on his ass. Chris managed to keep his feet under him and picked up the pace to a lead-footed trot, expecting at any moment to feel the hot chrome of the fender press into his lower back.

The burbling machine pushed him toward the edge of the property where a low barbed wire fence teetered amid the tall grass. Chris swerved off the driveway, summoning all of his sun-stroked strength into what could almost be called a sprint. He broke away with everything he had in him. He ran in a wobbling drunken monkey route, keeping his eyes on the tree line. If he could vault the fence and make the trees, they would have to follow him on foot.

Chris summoned to his mind the clearest image he could muster of himself springing over the barbed wire, majestic as a deer, though that image was immediately followed by another of falling belly-first onto the barbs, puncturing himself, becoming tangled, gouging his stomach on a rusty twist of steel.

The truck revved and raged past him on the left then swung around to cut him off. Chris tried to adjust course, to veer himself around the truck but he lost his footing and skidded sideways, spilling over onto his right haunch, skinning a slab of flesh from his elbow on the packed earth.

The truck stopped. The Driver got out, a gleaming black pistol in his hand.

The passenger door swung open.

"Stay in the damn truck!" shouted The Driver. He stalked to where Chris lay panting and coughing in the grass. The Driver pointed the gun at Chris's face. The barrel twitched aside and exploded with light and noise. Dust burst

62

into the air at Chris's elbow and the stink of gun smoke stung his nostrils. He flattened himself, pushing his face to the ground. His ears rang. Crows in the surrounding trees screeched in agitation and shook the foliage as they took flight. It took a moment for Chris to realize he had not been hit.

A boot pressed into Chris's shoulder and rolled him onto his back, pinning him there. The smoking barrel gaped in his face. The Driver was a shadow against the fading blue-gray sky.

"You stay on the road."

Chris spat a thick string of phlegm into the air.

A barrage of deafening noise cast up a cloud of dust and plant matter. Six shots in rapid succession burst right next to Chris's head. His skull rang like a bell and his heart pounded in his chest. His limbs locked, freezing with an overwhelming surge of adrenaline. His fingers were rigid claws in front of his face. An uncontrollable shaking took over his body, starting in his hands, then spreading down to his elbows until his arms shook before him.

Through the ringing tinnitus, the muffled intonation of the Truck Driver: "I shouldn't have to tell you the rules."

The Driver headed back to the truck and

climbed inside.

Chris inhaled deeply and slowly, imagining himself becoming pliable. First his fingers, then his arms, his legs, his neck. He would master himself. He would. He felt the tension evaporate from his body. The ringing tapered off.

Chris pushed himself to his feet and the truck inched forward, herding him back to the roadway.

***

The men drove him on for miles. Off the property and onto a narrow forest road. The sun fell, the sky a roaring orange through the tree-tops, like the whole world was aflame. The moon rose, a jaundiced hue behind a thin screen of drifting smoke.

Chris would stumble, fall, push back up with bloody hands, and jog along, his feet heavy, his head thoughtless, his wounded ankles a swollen agony. His vision narrowed and blurred. At times he would go completely blind, the black smudges at the periphery of his vision closing in to obliterate the world, and he would inevitably plant a foot into a divot in the road and tumble, or crunch directly onto a pine cone with a shredded sole.

64

At times, he would veer violently to one side or the other like a wino.

Darkness came fully. The headlights cast a long and distorted shadow before him.

Down, down, down they went into the valley depths, then up, up, up the twisting route that carved the mountainside. Always they kept him at the absolute limit of his speed, always the Ford pressed in on him, the heat of the grille like the breath of a dragon on his back.

Chris fell again and this time could not raise his hands to break the fall. Limp, he hit the gravel face-first. His only awareness was of the coolness of the road on his chest and cheek.

Brakes squeaked. The truck crunched to a stop. Doors clicked open. Voices. Unintelligible.

A new voice, coming closer, becoming clearer: "-stopped sooner, you kill them this way. You push them too far." The tone was soft but insistent, a pleading quality.

Gravel rasped. Chris felt a presence beside him and saw brown hiking shoes.

The man squatted and a face swam into Chris's churning vision. The new man had a lined, down turned face. He looked about fifty, with drooping, heavy brows, and jowls creasing around the mouth, a look like a basset hound, either sympathetic or pitiful. The head was ban-

65

daged and even in his stupor, Chris realized this man with the sad face was the one he had struck with his ax at the clearing.

"He dead?" asked the Driver.

"No," said Sad Face.

"Alright then, let's take him back."

"You should let him ride. He's pretty fucked up."

The boots of the Truck Driver stomped into view. Chris looked up. Those close-set eyes met his. The Driver signaled to the Mustache Man. Chris heard more boot falls, then his head was lifted roughly and a length of rope was looped about his neck.

The Driver climbed back aboard the truck, revved it up, and swung the vehicle to face back the way they had come.

Chris's wounded hands burned. Sad Face tapped Chris on the face.

Crunch of footsteps, a rustling noise, then more steps. A vehicle door creaking and then slamming shut.

Sad Face cradled Chris and helped him to a sitting position. His blue eyes met Chris's for the first time: a despairing look, the creases about that frowning mouth were cast in deep shadow, his cheeks catching the red light from the truck's rear end. Then he trotted to the Driver's win-

66

dow, hopped up on the running board, and clung to the window frame. Chris couldn't make out any words over the burping muffler.

A length of hairy yellow rope ran from Chris's neck to the trailer hitch on the back of the truck.

The Driver was speaking now, unseen, Sad Face staring into the cab with those puppy eyes. He dropped back off the runner, toward the back of the truck, put a foot up on the rear tire, and heaved himself into the box.

Chris feared they would drag him so he rose to his knees. Blood rushed and pounded in his temples. He fell sideways, rose again to all fours, and stared at the ground while his dizziness settled. The exhaust made him want to puke.

The truck growled forward, yanking the rope taut and pulling Chris onto his belly, the rough ground further abrading his bloodied bare chest.

The truck stopped and the Driver leaned out his window.

"Up!"

Chris seized the rope in both hands and used it to pull himself forward, shimmying on his knees. He grasped the knob of the hitch and pulled himself woozily to his feet.

The truck lurched, almost jerking him off his feet again, but he kept himself semi-erect and chugged along, holding the bulb of the hitch, bent almost double, his head heavy as a boulder.

Now and then he would manage to lift his gaze. Through the red glare he saw the black shadow of the man with the sad face watching him.

Chapter 11: Core Temperature

Chris knew he would die. They'd killed him.

The men left him lying in the dirt behind the truck, staring up at the glow of the smoggy moon. The Mustache Man unwound a length of garden hose from a plastic wheel on the side of the house to a decrepit shed. He then marched back and forth, stomping from one building to the other with an ice bag hanging in each hand, three, four trips.

The Driver and the Mustache Man hoisted Chris up by the legs and armpits. He was carried, swinging between them like a hammock, into the shed. It smelled of old lumber and gasoline. In the center of the space was a metal tub like a drinking trough for cattle. They swung him back and forth and heave-hoed him into the water.

The ice-cold impact slammed Chris like he'd been thrown onto a concrete slab. The air left his lungs in one mighty burst. His chest constricted and he cried out involuntarily. Chris shot into a sitting position, gasping. He managed to settle himself by clasping his hands to the stinging cold rim of the tub, wracked by wet coughs that tore at his throat.

The Mustache Man was laughing. Sad Face watched from the doorway with that defeated look that seemed etched into him. The Driver stood like a statue.

Eventually, the coughing subsided. Chris shook uncontrollably. He was gripped by a rapturous realization: there was water all around him. He scooped handfuls into his mouth with abandon.

"Might not want to drink so much of that," taunted the Mustache Man. "Make yourself sick."

"Let him," said the Driver.

Mustache Man shrugged. Sad Face shifted in the doorway like he wanted to speak but the Driver shot him a look and he remained silent.

Chris drank. He felt the cold pour into his chest and felt the water trickle into his stomach. With shaking hands, he scooped and scooped, slurping with total abandon. It hurt his teeth but it was a sweet relief to his tongue.

A wet rat scurried by the tub.

Sad Face left.

***

It was a mistake to drink the water. His teeth clacked painfully, his breath came in sputters, he grunted and hiccuped. The Mustache Man sat on a rickety bench nearby looking bored, occasionally snorting with laughter.

Chris clenched his jaw, trying to still the chattering of his teeth. His jaw hurt, he had a horrible sinus headache and he was chilled to the core. He could not hold still and went back to rattling like dice in a cup. His legs jerked. Chris banged his knees against the side of the tub. A stinging sensation had started in his fingertips and crept slowly inward, the fingers going numb until he felt only a cold burning in his palms and wrists where he gripped the trough's edge.

Most of the ice had melted. Only a few cloudy, smooth marbles remained bobbing in the water. The water was swirled with the mixture of bile and water he had vomited with torturous stomach contractions. His gut cramped and squelched.

Chris stared at the Mustache Man, who did not return his gaze. The guardian looked at the floor, eminently bored. He picked at a twig, splitting it into tiny pieces that he flung about the room. After a while, he looked up.

"What?" he said.

Chris vibrated, fighting to hold eye contact despite his tremors. He was determined to stare with as much malevolence as he could manage

71

in his horrid state.

"Quit fuckin' starin' at me, faggot."

The Mustache Man threw the remnants of his twig aside and rose from his seat.

There was a knock at the shed door. The voice of Sad Face came through the battered wood: "If you don't get him out of there soon, you lose him."

Mustache Man sighed, looked at Chris a moment, then strode to the tub.

"Dumb fuck," he muttered.

Chris was unsure if the comment was meant for him or the man outside.

More forcefully now: "Up. Come on, get out."

It was impossible. Chris knew, and he did not doubt the Mustache Man knew too. He couldn't even hold himself still, let alone raise his one-hundred and eighty pounds from the tub. He had no control of his body.

Mustache Man blew a long sigh. "Jesus fuckin' Christ."

He hooked his forearms under Chris's armpits like a forklift and heaved.

Chris felt body heat, the warm breath of exertion at the top of his head. His butt lifted from the bottom of the tub. Then he dropped again.

"Don't just bitch out there," called the Mustache Man. "Help me."

72

The door whined on its hinges and Sad Face entered. The two men hauled Chris over the edge of the tub and plopped him onto the filthy floor.

"Grab his legs."

Mustache Man took him by the armpits and Sad Face took up his legs at the knees. They carried him like a rolled-up carpet to the farmhouse. Chris spasmed and shivered in their arms.

In the basement cell, Sad Face wrapped him in a musty blanket and Chris huddled into a cocoon, wracked by shivers.

"You know," said Sad Face, "you should probably rub him all over if you want to warm him back up."

"Fuck you," spat the Mustache Man.

Sad Face disappeared for a time while the other man loomed over Chris with a look of total disgust.

Presently, the sad man returned with a steaming tin mug. He crouched down by Chris, said nothing, just held it out. Chris took the cup. It was water, warm enough to steam but not too hot.

"Sip it slow," was all he said.

73

Chapter 12: Shit Pail

When his legs were bound together, it had been tricky to squat over his toilet pail. Chris had learned, in his initial weeks, to brace himself against the wall so he wouldn't lose his balance while defecating. After the ice bath, they left his raw, chafed ankles unbound and he felt a freedom in this new ability to hold a wide stance. Small luxuries.

Sad Face had spent considerable time tweezing pebbles from the soles of Chris's feet, rinsing grit from the bloody rings around his ankles, dabbing them with ointment, and wrapping them.

Chris spent his time lying about, dozing. He was so worn down he need not worry about boredom or restlessness. His body needed to heal and he let it take control. No frustrating attempts to track time, not even any real fear of the future. Just fatigue, bodily functions, and lots of sleep.

In his waking intervals, Chris would stare toward the dim outline of the door. He felt that some part of his brain was scheming - or wanted to - but he had no conscious thoughts of escape. He was too tired, too fried. It was a strange sort of patience. He knew if he were to fight or break out, he'd need his legs and feet to heal.

The sad man came periodically to change his bandages under the watch of the Mustache Man. Every few days, Chris figured, based on how gross the wrappings became before they were changed. But who knew? Less often, the mustached guardian would come alone with a plastic tray or paper plate of food scraps, bread crusts, stringy bits of fat, chicken bones with little meat left on them, and a bottle of water. He'd take Chris's shit bucket with a look of revulsion and bring it back rinsed nominally clean.

Sad Face treated him in silence, the eyes always apologetic. Chris began to wonder if maybe this basset hound of a man was like himself, a captive, perhaps so broken by his ordeal that he'd turned collaborator. About the Mustache Man, he had no such quandary.

He felt pity for Sad Face. For the others, he felt a confusion and hatred that would flare to impotent rage. He would stare at the door and fantasize about killing them both. He thought about killing the sad man, and despite his pity felt few reservations. It may be something he needed to do, and, he mused, it could be a favor to the pitiful man.

Chris had known vile men before. He knew

75

the sadism that coursed inside of some. He thought of the cops who'd chatted nonchalantly while teenage Chris had sat in the back of the squad car, crying silently, fearing his arm would be amputated. He remembered how they had laughed with the paramedics when they arrived, how the medics had comforted him with a labored formality rather than any real warmth.

While changing his ankle bandages for what would turn out to be the last time, Sad Face gave Chris a long and meaningful look but said nothing. Chris felt like the man was trying to beam him a message, brain to brain.

***

Chris sat cross-legged in the dark, picking at the dry, cracking skin around his nails, occasionally peeling off a painful strip that bled. He also chewed at the insides of his cheeks, sucking them in and biting off bits with his canines and molars, now and then digging a finger in there to scrape away a troublesome flap with a nail.

A key scraped in the lock. Chris scrambled to his feet. He'd moved his shit bucket from the far corner. It sat beside him now. He snatched it up and stood back at what careful deliberation and vivid visualization had told him would be the optimal distance.

It had been some days at least since Sad Face had last doctored him. His ankles were almost fully healed and he imagined the other two brutes would keep the gentler man away from now on. Care was given at a minimum, as needed; cruelty was constant.

He'd refrained from shitting until his stomach hurt. The Mustache Man came more than once to check the bucket, finding it empty with barely concealed relief. Then when Chris could bear it no longer, he loaded up the pail as much as he could. After that, he chugged all of his water and rather than peeing in the drain, went in the bucket instead, swirling it around to mix the contents into a runny slime of uniform consistency, like pudding.

He was ready.

The door swung open and there was his mustachioed nemesis, alone, with a liter bottle of water and half of a Styrofoam takeout container of stale hot dog buns and spoiled bits of produce.

With a scream, Chris hurled the contents of his bucket. The jailer cried out. Chris charged ahead, swinging the plastic pail around to bash his enemy in the face. He got some shit on himself but could not have cared less. He charged

77

like a lineman, dropping a shoulder, slamming into the Mustache man, and knocking him clear across the hall. The other man sprawled onto his backside and smacked his head against the far wall.

Chris shouted again and kicked him in the crotch with all his might before bolting for the stairs. Daylight radiated around the rim of a door atop a half-flight of rough wooden steps.

The Mustache Man howled with rage.

Chris took the ladder-steep stairs two at a time, once faltering to bash his shin, his eyes set on the exit to freedom. He hit the door with a thud and a crack. He grabbed the handle and pulled. The door did not budge but strained at his jerking. He shouldered the door, feeling the dilapidated wood give. Then he yanked it back, slammed into it, yanked again, slammed.

A grip took his ankle and pulled. The stairs were gone from under him. His chin smashed against a plank, his teeth cracked together. An edge impacted his chest and took the wind from him. He slid backward, scraping his chest and belly on the rough wood.

He hit cold concrete in a daze. A steel-toed boot struck Chris in the crotch so hard the pain shot up into his abdomen and he threw up. His kidnapper was all over him, booted feet striking his head, his ribs, his elbow, knocking him senseless with a hoarse stream of obscenities. The reek of shit filled Chris's nostrils. He cried out in frustration, despair, and pain. Then the police baton came down on him all over, bruising his shoulder, smashing against his collarbone.

Chris kicked blindly and struck a shin. Then he was lost in a heart-stopping, hair-raising jolt of disorienting pain. He heard the insect-like buzzing of the taser, smelled burning hair and ozone. His jaw became locked in a painful clench.

The Mustache Man struck again with the taser. Any breath in Chris's lungs, any impulse in his brain was blasted out of him.

His legs were grabbed roughly and he felt the constriction of a zap strap, then another one. More blows to the head and body with the baton. Ties around his wrists now.

"God fucking damn you," cried the Mustache Man. "You fucking animal!"

The furious jailer stomped away, returning presently to take Chris roughly by the hair. A sticky band of darkness covered his eyes. Chris heard the scream of unwinding duct tape as the Mustache Man wrapped him around the whole head like a mummy. He could barely breathe. As the Mustache Man worked, he would periodically retch and gag.

Chris was seized again by the ankles. He managed a clumsy two-legged kick and was greeted with blows to the head, face, and neck in return. Then he was dragged.

His groin was inflamed with sickening pain.

He smelled the shit sprayed in his attack and felt himself dragged through a cool, wet smear on the concrete. The light changed from the dimness of the hall to the darker ambiance of the cell. A heavy rag was dropped over his face. It stank of fuel.

Then he was drowning. Gasoline poured, glugging from a jerry can. Chris tried to twist away. He was suffocating. The fuel burned his mouth and nostrils. It stung his eyes. Panic gripped him. It seemed to go on forever.

The stream mercifully ended and with a hollow sound like a bongo drum, the plastic can bounced painfully off Chris's head.

Chris rolled to his side. It took several hard shakes to get the rag off his face. He gasped for air and coughed. He had inhaled fuel in his terror. His throat burned.

He heard, then, the voice of the Driver.

"That's enough."

Another kick impacted Chris's crotch and he

retched, beset by a coughing fit.

"A'right, a'right." The Driver sounded amused. "Go get cleaned up. You fucking stink."

"God damn you," said the Mustache Man. Then he sniffed and stomped off.

The Truck Driver laughed.

Chapter 13: Stress Position

They'd kept him like this so long he'd shit himself. He couldn't help it. When the Mustache Man found him like that, he muttered "fucking disgusting" and left, returning after a few minutes with a hose fitted with a high-pressure nozzle. He blasted Chris's backside. It hurt his asshole but worse was the battering of the water against his swollen, discolored testicles. Mustache Man had smashed them so horribly they were still a glowing hell of agony. Occasionally the pain would flare up, seemingly out of nowhere, so bad Chris would grit his teeth and moan. Days (he thought it was days...) prior, he'd thrown up from it.

At least the dogs were gone now. When they'd taken the dogs away he thought it was over, that they'd leave him be and maybe send Sad Face to tend to his balls.

They came in rounds, the dogs brought in one at a time, held on choke chains barking in his face, so close he could smell the breath, feel its heat and splatters of drool on his face.

The pit bull had a mouth so big it looked like it could swallow his head whole, crush his entire skull from crown to jaw with one bite from that gargantuan, smiling mouth.

The rottweiler barked incessantly, a rapid-fire barrage that made his head hurt.

The shepherd he hated the most. By the time they brought in the shaggy shepherd dog for a round of screaming at him, Chris was so worn down by the previous two that he had no defense against the associations the breed brought to his mind, no escape from a flood of memories: it was like he was there again, laying under the parked car, childish fear coursing through him, when the dog scurried in, snapped onto his arm and yanked, tearing his flesh while he screamed...

After a time, his right arm actually hurt, his wrist ached and his hand felt numb. The horror was not just psychological but manifesting physically.

Chris had panicked then, and he was not in a position to panic. He was bound wrists to ankles behind his back, his chest pulled tight, his neck and shoulder muscles burning. It was already a struggle to breathe. To hyperventilate in such a position was a loss of control beyond anything he could have imagined.

After they'd gone with the German Shepherd and left him there, bound, hog-tied, his hip bones digging into the concrete, shoulders in-

83

flamed, he'd been overcome by the worst humiliation he had yet experienced. They had won. They had broken him. Chris had let them see, let them in. Up to this point, he had been quietly defiant. But now they had him. He had almost wept under the barrage from the shepherd. He almost wept now.

***

Memories came to Chris freely. Perhaps in his haggard state, he could see no future, and so his mind free-associated, drifting, memories swirling in intersecting eddies that plunged into nothingness.

It hurt to piss. Chris relieved himself where he lay, not even bothering to get up and move toward the drain. He lay on his side staring at the hole in the center of the room and his urine ran in a stream toward the drain, swooping almost all the way around it before trickling in. The fluid was tinged with blood, coming out with coral-pink ribbons that would mix in and tint the little river a sickly orange, which would then pick up dust from the floor as it flowed, becoming brown.

One of his wandering hikes in search of a place to camp had taken Chris through an aban-

84

doned mining site, where a pond was made oily and discolored by chemical runoff. The water shimmered with pastel streams of pink, teal, cerulean, and lime green. The surface pulsed with low waves encased by the oily membrane.

Two dead mallards spun bill-to-tail, black eyes in darkly iridescent green heads, turning against each other in a morbid yin-yang.

Chris was there again, really there, but this time instead of wearing hiking boots and track pants and shouldering a heavy pack, he was naked, his feet caked in the dirt of the trail. The ducks spun faster and faster, pulling the indigo streamers around and around into a whirling vortex, so fast the twin fowl seemed to blend together. Chris couldn't tell where one ended and the other began. They were united, a spinning wheel. And between them opened a drain, a black hole criss-crossed by a grid of metal.

Flies swarmed from the drain and a fetid stink arose. The hole grew bigger and bigger, rimmed by a swirling rainbow of day-glow poison, the gaps now big enough for him to fit through. Chris descended, pulled down like a flushed turd, into oblivion.

Through the darkness floated the humanoid caricature of the Bobblehead. He sat on a high-backed throne with brazen dog heads crowning the top and the arms. His brown robes were like the garb of an impoverished priest-king of some decadent fiefdom. Fighting dogs encircled the throne, floating in a rotating crown of pandemonium. Hundreds of them, thousands, a mandala of violence growing denser and denser, the animals duplicating, splitting like amoebas, each dueling pair becoming smaller but the mandala itself spreading wider and wider through the unending darkness. As the swarm grew, their king on his throne grew too.

The Bobblehead raised a knobby clawed hand and beckoned.

"Come."

Chris jerked awake and thrashed about in a panic, thinking he was still bound wrists-to-ankles. He smacked the knuckles of a free hand against the floor of the cell. He was lying much closer to the drain than before. Flies buzzed unseen in the darkness and taunted his ears. He moved back, panting, beads of sweat cold on his forehead.

"Shit," he breathed. "Shit."

Chapter 14: Kill Shelter

The men led Chris from the basement and across the property. He was blind in his sack, his hands tied before him. He stumbled occasionally on divots, stray pine cones, and dead branches.

The dogs ran laps around them, barking. Try as he might, Chris could not keep himself from jolting when one would bark particularly close to him, sometimes so close he would feel the hot breath on his balls and his stomach would drop in his abdomen.

He heard wooden clunking and scraping, followed by a jangling such as was made by a chain link fence. The feel of grass was gone from under his feet. Now he walked on packed earth. Wherever he was, it smelled of body odor and feces, with undercurrents of dust and dry bird shit. The ubiquitous smell of wildfire smoke was stronger since he'd last been outside.

A hand shoved him to his knees and the hood was jerked from his head. Chris blinked in the sunlight. The sun blazed behind a haze of xanthous smoke, bathing the world in eerie light like a decayed silent film.

Next, the straps on his wrists were cut loose. Chris was in the courtyard of a dough-

87

nut-shaped building built of wood and concrete, with a sloping roof of corrugated metal.

The dogs ran around the perimeter of the yard, stopping periodically to bark into one of the dozen dark, cage-doored cubbies that ringed the space. The cubbies were low, barely taller than the dogs.

The layout reminded Chris of a storage complex where he had slept in his brother's rented locker until they'd had a falling out. Later, his brother snitched to the landlord, who sent Chris packing with furious epithets and threats of calling the police.

The Truck Driver and the Mustache Man stood by Chris as Sad Face walked the perimeter undoing padlocks on some of the barred doors of the cubbies while bypassing others. Four in all were opened. Occasionally he would grab one of the dogs by the collar to keep it from charging into the tiny space. The canines were clearly excited, leaning down into play-invitation crouches yet barking with menacing savagery.

Sad Face returned, fixing Chris with one of his pleading looks, then glancing away as if ashamed.

Then the trio left, the Driver summoning the dogs after them with barked orders of "come!"

The chainlink inner gate clanged shut behind

88

them and they stood looking in. Mustache Man lit a cigarette.

A small sound caused Chris to whip his head back toward the opened cubbies. There was movement now in the shadowed boxes, tentative probing limbs. He saw a set of arms materialize in the central doorway, then a face floating above in the darkness. From another cubby, a scraping noise. His eyes darted several spaces over and he saw a figure scamper out.

It was an emaciated man with a ragged, clumpy salt and pepper beard. His face and nude body were blotchy, disfigured by what Chris realized must be horrible burn scars. An arm looked like the gnarled branch of some diseased tree, wrapped in a bark-like sleeve of twisting scar tissue. One of his eyes drooped half shut under a melted brow. Half his head was bald, bearing a palm-sized topography of calloused flesh. His genitals were fused into a tumorous mass of scar tissue that barely moved between disfigured thighs. He hunched in an ape-like crouch outside his cubby, eyes locked on the unknown newcomer.

A few doors down, a second man emerged. He was almost bald except for a horseshoe of sparse, spiraling ringlets that trailed greasily down his neck to the shoulders. At the crown of his skull, a few sad wisps blew in the hot breeze. He brushed them from his face with the spastic gestures of a dirt-caked hand. His limbs were scrawny and knobby at the joints, his ribcage prominent above a distended potbelly.

As if emboldened by the neighbors, two more men crawled from their pens. The first was missing nearly all his fingers, possessing only the thumb and index finger of his right hand and the pinky and ring finger of the left. He regarded Chris only briefly before directing his gaze to the saffron sky. Contemplating this for a moment, the man dropped his eyes to the dirt at his feet, where he traced a swirling path through the dust with his only remaining index finger.

The last to emerge trundled out lazily. He was easily the biggest, stocky and barrel-chested, his legs thick. Unlike the others, he stood straight once outside of the cubby. Even from this distance, it was clear he was considerably shorter than Chris but he was the only one that bested him in weight and muscle mass. His body was marred by a few scars, including one on the belly that left a slash through his pubic hair and stopped dangerously close to the pendulous genitals. He seemed the healthiest of the group, with a full beard of bushy copper. The only tell of his abject state were several nails on one of his feet that stuck out at painful angles from puffy tubes of green and purple flesh.

The crack and hiss of an opening beer can sounded from where the captors stood beyond the gate.

These quick impressions, gleaned in less than a minute, were all Chris had time for. The man with the burn scars was loping toward him in a monkey bounce. Two of the others shuffled about and moved closer. The one without fingers stayed where he was, intensely focused on drawing his spiral grooves in the dirt.

Chris stood tall and backed up a few paces. Burn Scars was picking up speed now. Chris widened his stance, getting low and bracing himself. He caught the charging attacker in a clinch and tried to throw him but the disfigured man was possessed of a surprising strength. He clung to Chris and managed to wrap a leg around one of Chris's causing both men to spill into the dirt together.

Baldy became excited, panting and grunting and dancing in closer.

Chris straddled Burn Scars and struck him twice in the face before the melted man got hold of Chris's wrists with a painful grip. Chris drove his knee into the buttocks and then struck home, planting a knee into the distorted mass

91

that had been the man's genitals. A moan came from the drooping mouth and the grip on Chris's wrists slackened. He jerked his left arm free and slammed a fist down on the face, driving knees into the crotch and glutes all the while.

But now Baldy had leapt into the fray, grabbing a fistful of Chris's hair with one hand and clawing at his jaw with the other, trying to hook fingers into the soft flesh behind the bone. Jagged fingernails cut tissue. Baldy pulled like he was trying to rip the head from the interloper's shoulders.

Finding it useless and painful to resist, Chris gave way, allowing himself to be pulled from the dazed Burn Scars. He then shoved backward with all his might, slamming his body to the dirt and pinning Baldy behind him. Chris threw elbows back into that distended gut. The bald man-animal bit him on the shoulder and he cried out. The fingers released his jaw and groped for his eyes. Chris grabbed one hand with both of his and bit as hard as he could. He tasted dirt, grime, and he dared not guess what else. Soon he tasted blood.

Chris rolled away, managed to extricate himself from Baldy, and scrambled to his feet, holding a wide, squatting stance like an Olympic grappler.

The one with the red beard circled wide. Chris marked him and realized with dismay that the man had moved almost ninety degrees around the courtyard while Chris was too busy to notice. Stupid of him to lose track of one of them like that. Fortunately, No Fingers had not moved from the spot just outside the door of his cubby, tracing crude fractals in the ground.

Burn Scars was on his feet now, then so was Baldy. Chris leapt toward Burn Scars and shoved him in the chest with both hands, slamming him to the ground, before turning in time to wallop Baldy across the face with a right hook. Baldy staggered back, then came at him again. Chris caught him by the throat, hooked a leg behind one of his, and slammed him to the ground. Then in one swift motion, Chris stretched up-ward, drew a knee up to chest height, and slammed his heel into Baldy's face.

He felt a crunch as the jaw gave way under his foot. Baldy went limp.

Immediately Chris was struck on the side, a blinding tackle slamming him to the dirt. Burn Scars was atop him. They grappled and thrashed about. The burned man took the top position and tried to bite him but Chris got a knee between their bodies and a palm against the melted forehead, holding him at bay. Burn

93

Scars waggled his tongue obscenely, a nightmare French kiss of gasping and grunting. Chris shoved out with arms and legs, sending the attacker falling backward onto his ass.

Chris scrambled to his feet and charged in to plant a swinging foot under Burn Scars' chin, sending him sprawling back with arms splayed.

Burn Scars rolled onto his belly and made to push himself up, but Chris fell atop him. He grabbed Burn Scars by what remained of his greasy hair and slammed his face into the dirt, then punched the disfigured man repeatedly in the back of the head, sending a shock of bone-on-bone impact through his forearm.

A thick arm, peppered with freckles, wrapped around Chris's throat. Chris felt stupid; he'd lost track of Redbeard again. Now he was locked in a choke hold. The stout, powerful man pulled Chris away from Burn Scars. Chris scrambled to keep his footing, stepping all over Burn Scars in the process.

He battled with Redbeard, the two men banging their legs together, trying to swipe the other's support from beneath him. Chris threw elbows, reached back, and grabbed the beard, pulling. Redbeard screamed and kneed Chris in the thigh, trying to fold him at the knee.

Chris's vision was tunneling, he huffed and

fought to draw enough oxygen. He slapped at Redbeard's head behind him with increasing feebleness. They sank into the dirt.

A piercing trill cut the air. The dogs howled. The Driver, the Mustache Man, Sad Face, and the dogs charged in. Mustache Man blew a referee's whistle.

"Drop him!" barked the Truck Driver.

The dogs circled in barking and snapping at Redbeard and Chris. The pressure on Chris's throat eased, the thick limbs released him, and he leaned on all fours coughing. Dogs barked in his face and he flinched away.

"Get back in there!" yelled the Driver, kicking at Redbeard, whacking him hard on the ass with a baton, a can of beer still in his other hand. Redbeard jogged away with harried, dainty steps, chased by two of the dogs, his pale butt cheeks jiggling. Chris was reminded of a gorilla running on two legs. Big Red crawled back into his cubby, peering out from the shadows. The dogs barked a few times at the threshold and then turned to run toward No Fingers, who scurried from them, abandoning his childish artwork to cower in his dark cubby.

The other two combatants lay where Chris had left them. Burn Scars was still. Baldy shook and twitched, white foam ringing his lips, in

95

some kind of fit or seizure. His eyelids flickered over white, rolled-back eyeballs. Sad Face crouched by Baldy.

Mustache Man and the Driver looked down at Burn Scars, then over at Sad Face.

"Well?" said the Driver.

Sad Face shook his head. His drooped visage imbued the action with a hopeless quality.

The Driver pulled a pistol from his belt and walked to Baldy. The compound rang with echoes of a gunshot. Birds swept up from hidden nooks and tittered their annoyance. The dogs barked and howled. They ran over to lap with eager tongues at the spray of gore that had burst from the top of the bald head.

"Put him away," said the Truck Driver, waving his pistol toward Chris. Then he waved the gun toward the bodies of Baldy and Burn Scars in turn. "And burn these."

He took a sip of his beer and walked out of there.

Chris sat in the dust and watched the feasting dogs jockey with each other.

Chapter 15: Mad Dog

Into his cubby, his new home. The cage door closed with a rattling of metal. Sad Face snapped the padlock shut. Chris knew this was intended as his home until death.

Six by six, with a four-foot ceiling. A cement box with a dusty cement floor sloping to a hole in the back corner. The raw-edged opening was intersected by a grate of rebar embedded in the floor and the cement around it was stained. Flies buzzed about. The stink pulled his upper lip into a sneer and caused his nose to crease at the bridge.

All in all, the space was similar to his basement cell, only much, much smaller. Chris could at most squat on his haunches. He couldn't even stretch out across the floor for push-ups. But through the bars was daylight. The sky. He wondered how often they'd let him out to stretch in the courtyard.

Sad Face hesitated before the bars, regarding Chris with that sagging mug of his. He looked like he wanted to say something but whatever it could have been, it was waylaid by the Mustache Man, who called out from the middle of the courtyard, "I'm not draggin' these fuckin' things

97

by myself!"

And those mournful ice-blue eyes broke away.

Later, Chris saw a dark pillar of smoke drifting up over the walls of the courtyard, arcing across a twilight sky the color of champagne. He smelled cooking meat and burning hair.

***

Despite the cramped quarters, Chris relished the cool night air, tinged only slightly with distant wildfire smoke. The fires must be well away yet, scorching some other part of the province. He wondered if a local evacuation order might lead to his rescue.

An owl hooted, crickets chirped, and he felt a quiet gratitude for these presences, these beings that were indifferent to him.

In the basement, Chris had felt humiliated and alone. The men treated him like an animal and it filled him with the fury of indignity. He thought of his autumn of camping, his winter at the motel, his dwindling funds, his return to the forest, the mornings waking up buried under a fresh snowfall...

Those had been hard times, sure, but sadness had been rare. Powerlessness even more so. Chris had felt more powerless at his job, in his apartment shouting through the ceiling at the landlord upstairs, begging friends for somewhere to crash. In the woods, at what was supposedly his lowest, Chris felt contemplative and at peace. He had a sense of proportion. At his campsites, he had relished every meager meal, and felt more satisfaction from setting up his tarps just so to cut the wind than he ever had from working for wages. He didn't feel misunderstood in a place where understanding was elemental.

Here, cross-legged on the ground, feeling the ache of his new bruises, his suffering felt timeless, the primeval horror of his predicament a condition of life stretching back unfathomably. Chris felt like an animal but an animal like any other and the world turned as it always had.

***

Chris decided he would try to speak to the other men. No Fingers, he knew, was nuts. Totally insane. But he had felt a vitality in the one he thought of as Redbeard.

Chris whispered, loud enough that he hoped his neighbor two doors down would hear clearly but not so loud as to carry beyond.

"Hey man, you there?"

Silence.

"You awake? My name is Chris."

He waited.

"I'm Chris," he said again.

He heard a faint shuffle. As he figured it, the man next door probably had not had anything one could call a conversation in months. Years, maybe.

So he continued: "What the hell is this? I didn't know there was anyone else here. I thought they were going to rape me or some shit... You there, man?"

A voice came to him then, a croak like a frog in the night.

"Dog shit," said Redbeard, and Chris winced, for the other man did not whisper, not even close, and Chris worried they would be heard from the house. "Dog shit. Fuck you! It's dog shit! You fuckin'... fuck you! Dog fucker! *Dog fuckers!*" The voice rose to a coarse shout. "He can see you! He knows you, he watches. Dog fucker. I'm a fucking *doctor.* I'll cut you open, *dog shit!* It's all it is! You don't know! You don't *know!*"

Somewhere out on the property, the dogs became agitated. They barked and Redbeard answered with barks of his own, lacing his animal

100

noises with strings of human obscenity.

Chris retreated into the shadows of his cage, certain that the men would be roused. He curled himself up on the gritty floor, ready to pretend to sleep, looking out through the bars at the night-stricken courtyard.

No one came.

Chapter 16: Machine Dream II (Grader)

Chris dreamt a memory. It was this:

When he was a boy, his father drove a snow-plow in the winter and a grader part-time in the summer. On a Sunday in June, he took his son out to teach him to operate the heavy machine.

Dad stood on the ladder and clung to the door frame, instructing the lanky, pubescent boy in the use of clutch and shifter. But young Chris didn't have the leg strength for the clutch. He was a late bloomer. He had not yet hit the growth spurt that would shoot him up and bulk him out later in puberty. He stretched his leg to push at the clutch with all his might but he had to flex his foot to depress it enough. He just didn't have the strength in his bony ankles.

The grader jerked forward heavily and stalled.

"You gotta press the clutch all the way down," his father said.

Young Chris tried again. The machine jerked violently forward and stalled out.

His father swung in the door frame, lost a leg out from under him, clawed at the door frame to stay on, and pressed a foot to the huge exposed tire tread.

"Fucking Christ," he said. "You're gonna kill me!"

It was supposed to be fun. They didn't have much fun together. But now Dad was upset. Chris rode the rest of the route, sitting on the dusty floor, as his father operated the machine along the gravel road in bitter silence.

Now Chris was an adult and his six feet and two inches was cramped on the floor of the tiny cab. His father's seat was empty. The cockpit smelled of hot plastic seat upholstery and of stale dust, which accumulated in a thick layer on the controls and piled in the corners of the interior. The windows were caked in filth.

The sky was black overhead and blazed Halloween orange behind the mountains. Over the horizon billowed a tower of brown smoke, reaching toward the threshold of the troposphere. At the top it gathered in a great ball, like a mushroom cloud, streaming taller and taller, the shaft growing thicker. It frothed and churned upward, a great tree of death, dwarfing the mountains, dominating the Earth.

Features congealed. A great bulbous head churned into crude facial features. A wide mouth split the bulb horizontally from one end to the other. Peaked ears rose like horns. The pillar below shaped itself in crude puffs and contortions, arms sprouted from the sides, and the smoke of the body smoothed out into great curtained sheets like flowing robes.

The rumble of the grader's diesel engine became a planet-shaking rumble of laughter.

Part III

Prize Winner

Chapter 17: Pig Barn

The tailgate came down with a squeak and a crash and the blackness was broken by sickly yellow light. Cool air swooshed into the stinking cargo compartment.

Chris had ridden for some time in the blackness, lying on his back in the box of the black Dodge under a tonneau cover, sealed in completely, alongside Redbeard and No Fingers. They were packed in like hot dogs in plastic, pressed together side to side. The air in the box swam with the thick stink of himself and his companions. During the ride, they had jostled and rolled together and apart, their warm, hairy naked bodies rubbing against one another. After a time, Redbeard's snores rose over the growl of the engine.

Despite his bound hands, Chris had managed to shake the black sack off his head. Now that the truck had come to a stop and the blade of light cut in through the rectangle of the open tailgate, he could see his fellow captives lying beside him, hands and legs tied, heads covered like inmates at Abu Ghraib. They were silent. Chris wondered if Redbeard was still asleep.

Calloused hands gripped Chris by the ankles

and tugged him from the truck box. He managed to plant his feet on the rough ground and stand as he came out. He squinted against the glare of electric lights beating down through the night. His captors were cast in silhouette. Behind them he could see a long, low building of corrugated aluminum. Away from the reek of his kennel mates, Chris's nostrils flared at the scent of pigs.

Vehicles were parked around in disarray. The light came from the steady glare of vehicle headlights and the swirling yellow-orange of burning metal drums. He heard a dull murmur of voices carried on the breeze from inside the building and the muffled bass throb of music.

The Ram was parked inside a fenced enclosure that formed a narrow walkway to an open cargo bay door leading into the building.

Cursing, pushing Chris to his knees, and slapping him across the face, Mustache Man leaned under the tonneau and emerged with the hood which he restored to Chris's head. Chris complied, a sense of dark curiosity overriding his foreboding. He was off the property, on new ground. Novelty at last after dreary months in the basement and the kennel, the bouts of torture, the isolation. It made him feel a mix of relief and a knot of fear in his gut.

The other men were subsequently pulled out,

allowing themselves to be slid like lumber and then descending compliantly to their knees.

The Truck Driver was some distance away speaking to a man in a leather vest with a long beard and a tattooed potbelly while Mustache Man bent along the row of captives, cutting their ankles loose with a pocket knife. Then Mustache Man ordered them up with little kicks in the ass and thighs, aided by verbal abuse.

Chris and his kennel mates shuffled out of the night and into the pig barn. An increase in temperature and a bizarre, horrible stink. Though evidently no longer in use for the keeping of livestock, the building still emanated the acrid stench of confined swine. The space was a confusing, unintelligible rabble of booming music, talking, shouting, jeering.

Chris tried to squint through the fibers of his bag... he could make out light and the movement of shadows but the material was too dense to see through.

He stumbled on a ledge, got his bearings, and found himself mounting his way up a metal ramp. He tripped again on a lip at the top and stumbled onto a flat area that was soft underfoot and smelled of sawdust. His hood was ripped from his head and Chris found that he was looking down upon a huge space falling to dilapidation and packed with men.

Dozens and dozens of men, a sea of bald heads, cowboy hats, leather caps, gray and brown and blond hair. A whiteboard of betting odds, shouting bookies trading cash for chits. It was a maelstrom of noise and images.

Chris felt queasy. The air pressed on him. The smell was like the kennel in the aftermath of the fight with Redbeard, No Fingers, Baldy and Burn Scars. Blood and fluids, sweating male bodies mixed with the barn's indelible pig-stink. The heat was sticky, the light swimming with motes of dust.

Chris, his kennel mates, and their handlers were in a kind of raised holding pen at the center of the space, surrounded by a waist-high fence of metal and connected to the loading bay by an enclosed path that split the crowd. In the center of the pen, two men in overalls worked to pile small and mid-sized boulders into a crude pyramid.

Across the enclosure, three more men, a similar cadre to Chris and his two companions, naked like them, were being shuffled up an identical ramp by handlers who wore denim, leather work boots, and ratty hats. The decrepit trio comprised an emaciated man with blond dreadlocks; a short, long-limbed man with a bul-

109

bous nose that looked like it had been broken countless times, and wide-set eyes that reminded Chris of a boy he had grown up with who had Fetal Alcohol Syndrome; and an older man with a bald pate ringed by strings of white hair, no ears, and a gaping purulent eye socket that showed necrotic pink and green flesh where the eye had been gouged.

Then the handlers all backed out with no fanfare, no instructions to their charges. The pen was closed with a clank at both ends, and there came two short blasts of an air horn.

"No more bets! No more bets! Time's up, boys! All bets placed!"

Chris understood where he was. He had the knowledge lurking behind his conscious awareness but now the full realization took hold, undeniable. The barn was a redneck Kumite dungeon and he knew this fight would be to the death, team against team, for the lustful, sadistic pleasure of the hooting rabble that packed the barn.

A hush fell on the crowd, followed by a single, long wail from the horn.

Redbeard, No Fingers, and the three opponents charged for the center of the pen in an immediate jostling clash for the stacked boulders, scrambling to grab a hefty one and bring it to bear against an opponent. Chris hung back and circled wide. The crowd roared.

No Fingers fumbled with a stone as big as his head, dropping it from his mangled hands. He was then struck hard, a cracking sound of stone on skull, audible over the noise of the crowd. No Fingers collapsed on the rock pile. The assailant, the emaciated man with blond dreadlocks, threw a rock down onto No Finger's head, leaving himself temporarily unarmed and slightly off balance.

Chris charged in, leapt the limp body of No Fingers, and tackled White Dreadie flat. Sawdust burst into the air, grating at Chris's eyes and nostrils.

A stinking body seized Chris in a bear hug and pulled him from White Dreadie. Chris stomped a heel onto the attacker's foot, threw back an elbow, and tore himself out of the clutch. He spun to face his opponent and saw Bulb Nose grinning at him with a mouth full of chipped, disgusting teeth.

Chris swung a kick out, not intending to connect, just holding some space for himself, fending off Bulb Nose and White Dreadie, who rolled to his feet with dangerous agility. Chris scooted and shuffled, staying mobile, never still, jabbing and kicking, occasionally connecting with an enemy body, and scanning the space.

In a corner of the enclosure, Redbeard squatted, a business-like expression on his face as he bashed in One Eye's head.

Bulb Nose threw a smallish stone at Chris. He dodged... mostly, catching a glancing blow to the shoulder. A starburst of pain radiated up his neck and down his bicep. Bulb Nose came on at full speed, knocking Chris down. The mush-faced enemy tried to gouge Chris's eyes with cruddy, yellow fingernails. Chris gripped him by the wrists.

White Dreadie charged in and began kicking Chris in the side. Jagged toenails cut him.

Redbeard plowed in from the side, sending Dreadie careening into Bulb Nose, toppling over him, and knocking the gouger off Chris. Red smashed a heel into Bulb Nose's crotch, and seized White Dreadie by the hair, yanking his head around. They grappled as Chris rolled to his feet, snatched up a rock, and brought it down onto Bulb Nose's face before the enemy could recover from the pain in his crushed balls.

Bulb Nose fell back, stunned, blood gushing from a split at the bridge of his nose. Chris bludgeoned him again, pulverizing his teeth. The jaw hung limp. Chris plunged the stone down again, grinding and mashing the face.

Red threw Dreadie, sending him careening toward Chris. Chris ducked down and Dreadie tripped over him and hit the metal barricade, bending at the waist and almost toppling over into the crowd. The spectators howled. Chris set upon his dreadlocked opponent with the gory rock he had used to pulp Bulb Nose, smashing Dreadie on the back of the head and neck with as many quick, successive blows as he could. The audience was pressed in all around them, a roaring, tumultuous sea of masculine hatred.

"Kill that fuckin' hippie!"

"Smash his head!"

"Fishhook him!"

Dreadie hung limp, bent over the barricade. A leg spasmed then he moved no more.

With the enemies dead, Chris dropped the rock and slumped, panting. He looked over at Redbeard...Who was charging at him with a rock upraised in two hands.

The crowd shouted malevolent joy. Chris jumped forward, bent low, hoping his opponent would come in too fast and he could get inside of Redbeard's strike range before the blunt weapon swung down to crack his skull. He bulldozed to Red's belly and felt the rock whump down onto his back. Chris dropped to his knees but he held fast and his momentum carried the stocky man onto his back.

They wrestled on the ground, grappling and scratching, trading off on the dominant position. Chris tried to put his kennel mate in an arm bar but the man managed to wriggle and get hold of Chris's arm. Red bit down just below the inside elbow, hard. Chris cried out. Blood ran from the wound to stain the copper beard with streaks of burgundy. Redbeard growled.

Chris punched him in the side of the head. Red pushed up to his feet, danced back, and seized a boulder, raising it in a freckled hand.

Chris rolled aside and got up onto his knees, cradling his wounded arm close to his body. Red threw his boulder and Chris scurried aside. The projectile smashed into another rock and split into three large shards. Chris grabbed one of the jagged wedges of broken rock as Redbeard ran at him. At the last moment, Chris moved aside and slashed out at that bulky body.

The jagged edge sliced a pinky-wide, ragged gash into Redbeard's side. Red made a hideous gasp.

Chris whacked him at the base of the skull and then swung his sharp fragment, slicing the other man across the side of the face, tearing a copper-bearded cheek open into a lopsided grin. Blood and chips of teeth sprayed across the arena. The impact sent the redhead tumbling backward to splay out on his back.

Chris fell on his former partner, plunged the rock wedge down into the man's mouth, shattering what remained of his teeth and nearly taking his head off at the jaw hinge.

Red spasmed and went limp. Hot piss streamed into the sawdust.

Chris rose, the stone wedge held in both hands. Blood ran from his forearm. His knees were raw, his shoulder burned, and there was already a green yellow blob of a bruise forming.

The crowd roared but over the rabble a distinct individual voice rose, coming closer, becoming clearer.

"I said drop it!"

The Truck Driver and the others were in the pen now, approaching Chris with batons.

"*Drop it!*" The Driver was shouting over the crowd. His eyes were locked on Chris, stern, like a scolding father. Chris looked at the rock, looked at Redbeard, and let the boulder fall from his hands to the wood dust.

"That's it," said the Truck Driver.

Chris's wrists were bound together. Before the hood came over his head, he saw men hopping the fence of the enclosure, some working in pairs to drag the battered corpses down the ramp while others threw down fresh sawdust.

***

Blinded by the sack, out of the rabble, into the cargo bay. Chris felt a set of hands on each upper arm. He heard the click of the tailgate opening and one of the men gripping his bicep – by the smell on that side, it was the Mustache Man – let go and then kneel in front of him. Chris felt a hand grab his ankles, pressing them together to bind them with a zap strap.

Chris struck out with a knee. He felt hard contact with a chin and heard a grunt. He threw an elbow into the gut of the man still holding him and twisted himself from the gripping hands. He bolted, blindly stepping and almost tripping on the man he had kneed. He pushed the mask from his face with bound hands.

By the time he jerked off the hood, he had already gathered blind momentum and he hit the waist-high fence encircling the loading area. He flipped head over heels and landed flat on his back, the wind knocked from him.

Chris drew a desperate breath, rolled to his belly, and forced himself up but the Truck Driver had already vaulted the fence. The prongs of a taser jabbed in beside Chris's lower spine. His breath ran from him and he was overpowered by a convulsion. He dropped to one knee. Drool ran down his chin. Another hit with the taser, in the neck this time. The Driver embraced him in a paralyzing choke hold.

"Stupid, stupid, stupid," said the Truck Driver.

Chris sputtered and squirmed. Over his shoulder he managing a glance at his subduer. He could feel hot breath on his neck, stubble scraping his cheek, the big, hot denim-clad body of the Driver pressing against his naked flesh. The Truck Driver pulled Chris up on vibrating legs and squeezed tighter. Chris kicked once but not in attack; it was an involuntary spasm of muscles. His legs turned to putty under him, his arms pulsed, his hands tingled and his vision narrowed to a pinpoint until he dangled in his captor's arms.

The Driver threw him down like a rag doll and kicked him hard in the back and ass, then stepped over him and kicked him in the gut.

The Mustache Man hopped over the fence, furious, blood trickling from his nose and a split upper lip. He kicked Chris in the chest, arms, and shins, brutally and repeatedly. Mustache Man and the Driver were in harmony, beating Chris in the dirt. Chris could do nothing, the impacts of the kicks taking over his whole body, losing any specific locality and transforming from pain into a sensation of spatial dissociation, disorientation, falling...

He could muster no strength to fight.

"Get him in the truck before anyone else sees this shit," spat the Driver.

Sad Face climbed the railing and helped Chris up. He and the Mustache Man hauled Chris over the fence. The Driver followed and stooped to pick up the bag, shoving it over Chris's head. He wrapped a zip tie around Chris's neck at the base of the sack, yanking it tight, sealing the bag below the jaw so Chris could not pull it off or shake it loose.

Chris was thrown at the back of the truck, landing half inside and smashing his kidney against the open tailgate. Mustache Man kicked at his legs and punched his buttocks and thighs. Chris squirmed up onto the truck bed like a caterpillar and curled in on himself, reeling from the choke hold and the electric shocks and the beating, from everything.

118

Chapter 18: Bugs

Crickets chirped in the still night air.

As the river of ants swarmed up his legs, onto his balls, his taint, into his ass crack, Chris tried to relax, to breathe as steadily as his taut chest would allow. This strategy bought him some time, but gradually his jaw clenched. He started to grind his teeth, and after who knew how long - probably not long at all - the only way to discharge the mental pressure was to moan.

Chris had enough presence of mind to know he didn't want to scream, didn't want them to hear him, so he groaned with his mouth clamped shut. His ass, legs, and abs were wracked by involuntary twitches and shivers that strained against his bonds. He fought to maintain discipline, to think of anything but the horrible itching of the army of little legs swarming on him, the occasional pinch of a bite. His shoulders were on fire. His mind was on fire. Mosquitoes tortured his ears.

They had returned from the pig barn in the early morning hours, as the birds sang to welcome the first flare of dawn and the clouds ignited like coals in a campfire.

Chris was lashed to a pole by wrists and ankles, his arms bent back, his knees in the dirt. About three feet from the ground, a rod jutted perpendicular from the pole, pushing Chris forward between the shoulder blades so that his arms were pulled to their maximum extremity. He leaned forward at an almost forty-five-degree angle. His breathing was labored, every inhale pressing the rod into his spine. He was only able to take only shallow breaths and soon became light-headed.

They'd tied him there as the smoke-stained red sun rose. The Mustache Man had menaced him with the dogs, letting them snap at his face, barking and snarling, their hot breath stinking, until the sun was high in the sky. Then he had been left to the heat of the day.

When the sun began to descend in the dirty sky, the men tormented Chris once more with the dogs, sprayed him with the hose, and whipped him about the abdomen and shoulders with long twigs scrounged from the yard.

As night fell, the Mustache Man poured off-brand pancake syrup all over him.

***

The chomps and nibbles that covered the most sensitive areas of his body itched terribly.

Chris had mosquito bites in his ears and terrible little sores on his penis and scrotum, the insides of his thighs, between his butt cheeks. His muscles hurt and his flesh was tender all over.

Chris would doze but then a spasm of leg or body would shake him awake, and he would thrash about, feeling the ghosts of insects swarming him. He'd been thankful when the Mustache Man had come at dawn to blast him again with the garden hose, freeing him from the creatures that crawled all over him, and soothing his irritated flesh with cold.

When his bonds were cut, he fell face-first into the dirt. Mustache Man dragged him to his cubby in the kennel.

Now Chris heard the sound of footsteps crossing the courtyard. A whispering patter of bare feet, not the usual clomp of boots, and coming fast.

From where he lay, knees tucked up, facing the back wall of his cage, he heard the quick steps getting closer. Chris heard breathing, someone there, crouched outside his cubby but he didn't look. The voice of the man with the sad eyes came to him in a whisper, quavering between regret and dark anticipation.

"Don't bolt. They'll kill you before you get a rep for bolting. You just have to survive. I'll get you out or I'll... we'll try. You just have to be patient... for now... and just... survive. Please."

They held a silent proximity for a while.

"I'm sorry."

He left.

Chapter 19: Power Tools

The opponent Chris faced was clearly terrified. The young man shook at the knees. He looked on the verge of tears. The long, youthful face was sunken and pocked with acne, the shoulder-length hair stringy with grease. Wisps of black hair adorned his chin and upper lip, the pube-like bristles of semi-manhood. He could barely lift the black and yellow DeWalt drill in his skinny arms.

The ruckus of the crowd was buried beneath the thunk of two-stroke motors. They were outside, on a slab of asphalt that poured like a lava flow from the gaping mouth of a derelict auto body shop. The yellow crescent moon was like a toenail clipping.

Chris and Pube Face circled each other. Chris was hesitant to make the first move, seeing how tremors wracked the boy, the nervous biting of the lower lip, and the shifting eyes. If it were up to Chris, he would let the poor kid walk. But it wasn't up to him.

A razor-fine jet of water stabbed Chris in the kidney like the point of a spear. He buckled under the sudden, penetrating pain, and spun away from it. Over the motor noise, the crowd hooted with demented enjoyment.

Pressure washers were spaced evenly around the ring, one at every 45 degrees of the circle. It didn't matter where the combatants were, they were vulnerable to the penetrating force of the pumps from all sides.

Several jets angled together to hammer at Chris's ass, back and thighs. He had nowhere to go but forward. As he was pushed ahead he saw the skinny young man being similarly driven toward him.

Pube Face set his face with a look of grim determination, revved the electric drill in his hands, and ran at Chris, thrusting the power tool.

Chris slid aside on the wet concrete and drove his foot into the back of the young fighter's knee. The teen spilled to the floor with a clumsy flailing of limbs. A jet of water smashed into the boy's face, breaking the skin of his cheekbone. He screamed and cowered.

Chris could have charged in and finished him but his own hesitance was abetted by streams of water from all directions battering his torso. A jet hit his throat and he tried to duck away from it. Another jet hammered his genitals and the pain was so intense he yelled. Chris feared his sack would tear. Jets struck his face, trying

124

to bullseye his open mouth. He clenched his legs together and covered his crotch with his free hand but doing so left his face exposed and the jets raked up his body to stab him there. A spear of water in the eye would surely blind him.

The crowd roared with laughter that blended with the clamor of the gas-powered pumps.

Pube Face rose up on bird-like legs, unharried by the painful streams that punished Chris. He charged in. Chris was half-blind in the spray. The kid shoved his drill toward Chris, whose feet slipped on the wet floor in an attempt to dodge.

Chris landed on his side, painfully cracking his elbow. He rolled to his back. The boy descended on him, power drill whirring. Chris kicked him in the thighs and the kid fell forward. The drill bit slammed into the pavement less than an inch from Chris's scrotum. Fierce jets of water impacted the side of his head so hard he thought they would scalp him. A spray hit Chris in the ear and he rolled away, fearing a ruptured eardrum.

On his knees, Pube Face groped desperately for his drill in the spray, hefted it up like a pistol, and pulled the trigger. Nothing happened. He thrust the dead tool at Chris like a knife. On his back, Chris kicked the drill from the oppo-

125

nent's hand, then struck out again, planting a foot square in the center of the kid's bony face.

Pube Face fell backward and Chris sprung up, straddled him, and smashed his own drill down like a war hammer on the young man's head. The plastic battery casing cracked. The adolescent fell back flat. Chris struck again but guilt and disgust held him back from his full strength.

The jets of water slammed his chest and face. Chris stood and backed away from the kid, fighting against the harassing power washers. He threw down his drill. Chips of plastic scattered about.

The men booed viciously. The kid writhed on the pavement, clutching his head.

All the jets concentrated on Chris. It was pain from all angles. The wet blades broke the skin of his glans, tore at his nipples, stabbed at his cheeks and ears. Chris thrashed his head about, struggling to cover too many sensitive spots at once. When he tried to cover his ears, they went for the eyes. When he tried to protect his eyes, they went for his cock and balls. When he covered those, it was the ears and face again.

He knew what they wanted.

Fending off the merciless high-pressure spears, Chris lurched to where the concussed boy lay. He knelt on the kid's throat, hunched over, tucking his chin to his chest against the painful water. He covered his head with one arm and his exposed asshole with the other and pressed the boy's windpipe until the jets stopped.

"Up," commanded the Truck Driver, striding onto the wet killing floor.

Chris rose and looked down at the kid he had killed, who could not have been more than 17 years old. He felt sick with guilt and shame, but more than that Chris felt a burning, pure hatred for the men that surrounded him. The hooting fools that tormented them with the pressure washers, the Driver, the Mustache Man... He cringed at the touch of his handlers as they strapped his wrists and bagged his head.

Chris felt the crushing inevitability of all things; the static, unyielding weight of the eternal present. An event could be impossible, unimaginable - until it occurred. But once it happened, that meant it was always going to happen, had always been there. In an instant what was impossible was the idea that things could ever have been different. What was done was done.

Chapter 20: Some Care

In the kennel, they fed him dog food. The Mustache Man would come with a Styrofoam bowl of wet slop. At first it made Chris gag. He couldn't bear to eat it but when Mustache Man returned the next day with a fresh helping and saw the uneaten brown muck in Chris's dish, he beat him severely. Then the dog food deliveries were withheld for days on end.

When his feeder finally returned, Chris was so hungry he scooped handfuls of the awful stuff, sucked his fingers, and licked the bowl clean. It was actually delicious.

The Mustache Man was very amused by this.

***

One evening the Mustache Man did not come. It was Sad Face. He had the usual bowl of lumpy chow but after he had passed it through to Chris - passing it into Chris's hands rather than tossing it in as the Mustache Man liked to do - he pulled a Ziploc bag from his pocket.

Crammed into the bag were half a hamburger patty, bits of chicken, a few slices of cheese, and a handful of what looked like scrambled eggs.

Chris could not take his eyes off this bounty. He had not eaten real human food since the early days in the cellar. At that time, he had been insulted and enraged by being fed table scraps. Now his mouth hung open and watered.

Sad Face reached into the baggy and scooped out a handful of the contents.

"I can't let you have the bag," he said. "They might find out."

He set the food scraps gingerly onto the concrete. Chris could not have cared less. He was enraptured.

"Look at me," said Sad Face.

Chris forced his eyes from the pile on the floor to the careworn face on the other side of the bars. Pale eyes under sagging eyebrows.

"You'll need strength for what's coming."

Chapter 21: Bodied

The rabble of voices grew louder as they marched Chris from the cool night air into a humid and raucous room. The noise swept over him like surf. Through the hood, Chris could see the white glare of spotlights, their dry heat palpable, cutting through and contributing to the wet body warmth of the crowd.

Chris heard an unfamiliar, gruff voice: "You for the three-two?"

"Yeah," responded the Driver.

"Pretty rough one you got there."

The men shoved Chris forward and pulled the hood from his head. He stood like a statue, an anemic David, to one side of a large hexagon constructed of bare wooden posts and chain link, festooned around the top with ribbons and tatters of fabric. The place stunk.

On either side of him, a few feet away, were other teams of handlers with their charges. One was a scrawny man a couple of inches shorter than Chris, so thin that his vertebrae protruded from his back. His chest was concave in the middle, his legs avian-thin and knob-kneed, his bare ass cheeks concave like his chest. The other man was short and round of head, with

130

a snaggle tooth protruding from his mouth, a loose, jiggling belly, and thick thighs.

Two men in overalls dragged a nude body from the hexagon by its legs, the smashed skull leaving a streak in the sawdust, while two others piled small boulders in the center.

There was a brief hush in the crowd, then a surge of joyous, baritone screaming. A gate clanked open at the far end of the hexagon and two crews of three men entered, each leading a huge fighter whose face was hidden behind a grotesque mask and whose neck was encircled by a spiked collar attached to a leash. Even after all he had been through, Chris was beset by a queasy terror.

The first was a towering barrel of a man, nearly seven feet tall, his body almost hairless and spider webbed with scars across his neck, chest, belly, and legs. His mask was of a blank expression, spray painted black, open below the nose with a window revealing a mouth of tiny teeth filed to points. But most striking of all was this: both of his arms were amputated below the elbow, and as Chris watched, his handlers strapped a blade to each stump. To the right stump, a short sword like a gladius, two feet long and straight-edged; to the left stump, a two-foot pole terminating at a wide crescent ax

131

blade like an oriental fan. The forearm stumps slid into sockets and the handlers tightened leather straps around the elbows. As the weapons were cinched tight, his huge circumcised cock became tumescent.

The second fighter was stockier, much shorter, with a gigantic, bald oval head that dwarfed a mask that retained the raw texture of tree bark. This man-beast was hobbled by a crooked, stomping gait, for at the end of one leg in place of a foot was an iron block like the head of a sledgehammer. His potbellied torso was covered in clumps of curly hair and his legs were so hirsute the effect was like some kind of fucked up satyr. His stubby, uncut dick was so small it peaked like a zit from a greasy nest of pubes.

While Blade Arms glared at Chris across the ring, grimacing to show off his fangs, Clubfoot wasn't looking at anyone, just the dusty floor, seeming almost shy, self-conscious of his mutilated freakishness.

The freak masters unclasped the leashes from the collars of their monsters.

The Scrawny Ass man to Chris's right whimpered and there came a pattering of piss hitting the sawdust.

The cage door slammed shut with a noise like a tambourine. A horn blared.

Chris's fellow captives stood frozen, backs to the fencing, but the two warrior-freaks marched forward with terrible purpose.

The chubby Snaggle Tooth to Chris's left said "fuck it" and charged for the central pile of rocks. He had only just laid a hand on one when Clubfoot took a crooked hop forward and kicked out with his hammer-leg. He caught Snaggle Tooth on the forehead with a hideous *blump* and the pudgy man splayed over backward, shaking and seizing, his scalp peeled back at the hairline, oozing blood.

Clubfoot staggered forward, raised his iron foot, and brought it down, pulverizing the cherubic face of Snaggle Tooth. The round head burst like an overripe melon, brain matter splattering out into the sawdust. The monster twisted his hips, grinding the head like he was snuffing out a cigarette.

Scrawny Ass ranted, "fuck fuck fuck fuck *fuck!*" He danced along the edge of the cage, bumping against Chris, pushing him sideways. Chris stepped aside, and the skinny dancer almost lost balance.

Chris's eyes swept from Blade Arms to Clubfoot. They were spreading out, getting in front of the rock pile, controlling the center of the cage. Chris needed to put distance between himself

133

and Scrawny Ass, not just to get away from a panicked and untrustworthy competitor, but to divide the attention of the killing machines. He feared getting close to Blade Arms but sensed some vulnerability in Clubfoot's lopsided slowness.

Blade Arms charged. Chris dodged to the right, collided with Scrawny Ass, and the two of them fell over.

"Oh my god, oh fuck," babbled Scrawny Ass.

Chris rolled up and scrambled away as their beastly opponent charged in. Blade Arms slashed down with his fan to open a shrieking Scrawny Ass from the throat to the belly button. Blade Arms plunged his sword into the chest just below the nipple. The shriek became a gurgle. The sword pulled free with a wet sucking. Blade Arms dropped to one knee and slammed the fan-blade into Scrawny Ass's throat, pushing almost all the way through with his initial thrust then tilting back and forth to saw through the spinal cord.

Chris saw his chance. He dodged around Clubfoot and slammed into Blade Arms from the side while his fan was still embedded in Scrawny Ass. Blade Arms staggered backward, swinging his arms for balance, catching Clubfoot with a glancing swipe of the gladius. Clubfoot howled and clomped backward, lost his lopsided balance, and fell on his ass.

Chris dashed for the rock pile, snatched the largest stone he could get his hand around, and threw it at Clubfoot. The rock thumped into the side of the bald head, drawing blood. Chris had another rock, launching his projectile now at Blade Arms, who raised his sword arm to protect himself and took the rock on the elbow, roaring with pain and anger. Chris threw as hard and fast as he could, desperate to hold the middle of the hexagon, overcome by an animal frenzy.

His chest burned with exertion, his knees strained from scooping and launching the heavy stones. His back was tight with pain.

Blade Arms had been driven into a corner. Chris threw another stone that slammed the freak in the forearm. Clubfoot could not right himself under the barrage: he reclined like some nightmare parody of a man at the beach, screaming, swinging his arms, howling in agonized confusion, the boulders colliding with his knees and forearms and shoulders.

The pile grew small, but the base had the biggest rocks. Chris heaved one up with two hands and charged toward Clubfoot, leaping over the mashed corpse of Snaggle Tooth, bashing the rock down against Clubfoot's egghead. Chris lost balance and fell atop the hot, greasy body, rolled off, picked up the rock, and hammered it down. Clubfoot's head burst with a horrid squelch, liquefied brain matter pouring out. Chris raised the stone again, thrusting it down with a cry. It splatted into Clubfoot's already smashed face and nestled in a crater of gore. Clubfoot lay like a starfish, the rock embedded in his face like a hardboiled egg in a cup. Blood oozed at the edges of the rock and clear slime seeped from cracks at the crown of the skull.

Blade Arms had regained his footing, bleeding from multiple wounds. His fan-blade was raised but his injured sword arm was cradled close to the body, a jagged splinter of bone jutting from what remained of his forearm. He let out a hoarse bellow and charged.

Chris prowled around the rock pile, leading Blade Arms almost a full circle to where Scrawny Ass lay decapitated. Chris snatched up the head and thrust it up just as the ax-limbed oaf struck. The crescent blade embedded in the stray head with a sickening thud. Having caught his enemy, and still fearing a swing of the sword, Chris kicked the mutant Goliath's genitals. The freak cried out.

Chris pressed his advantage, pushing the

136

monster back against the chain link, pinning the sword flat between their bodies, and holding the ax limb up high with the pitiful head. Red goop gushed from the severed neck stump onto the combatants, lubricating their struggling bodies.

The sword's edges cut into Chris's pectorals. But Blade Arms was fatter and the more Chris pressed in, the more the blade pushed back into its owner's flesh, slicing his breasts. Chris felt the heat of their fresh blood on his chest and the cooler streams from the head of Scrawny Ass, all of it mingling. He felt the bite of the blade.

His forehead was at his enemy's jaw level and he smashed forward with headbutts. The sharpened teeth cut into him and blood mixed with sweat to burn his eyes.

Blade Arms screamed and pushed against him, but Chris held on, twisting and wrenching at the fan arm to batter his opponent's head with that of the late Scrawny Ass. Chris kneed Blade Arms in the crotch then yanked at the head, which came flying loose and rolled away.

Before the enemy could get his bearings, Chris grabbed the prosthesis below the crescent blade and twisted it toward the behemoth's chest, driving his knee into the pendulous genitals all the while. The wide blade bit into the sword-mounted forearm. Pressing with all his weight, and kneeing frantically at the crotch and belly, he drew back and slammed in. The razor-sharp crescent pushed all the way through, the sword arm falling to the ground and the fan slicing into the fat chest.

Blade Arms howled.

Chris punched him in the face and kicked his leg out from under him. The monster tumbled and hit the dust.

Chris scooped up the severed sword limb. As Blade Arms twisted about, Chris came down, plunging the blade into the thick belly. Blade Arms burped yellow slime and loosed a wet moan. Chris stirred the blade about, scrambling the guts. The fat warrior thrashed, his fan blade gashing Chris across the shin.

Chris wrenched the weapon out and drove it into the chest. Blade Arms sank back with a squeaking exhalation like a deflating balloon.

Chris raised his face to the rafters and screamed.

He pulled the grotesque sword from his vanquished opponent with a squelch and stumbled backward.

A voice came, and he thought it was the voice of Bobblehead:

"Drop it!"

It was the Truck Driver.

138

"Drop it!"

With a casual fling, Chris sent the blade arm spinning like a boomerang toward his approaching handlers. It flew nearest to the Mustache Man, who flinched away from it. It clashed against the chain link enclosure and fell to the floor.

The Truck Driver stood too close to Chris and snorted out a little laugh. Chris could smell the liquor on his breath.

"You think you're real clever, huh, fucker?"

The Driver dropped the hood onto Chris's head while the Mustache Man took his wrists and bound them. They led him out amid the screaming pandemonium.

Blade Arms and Clubfoot's handlers dragged their hulking bodies out by the legs.

Chapter 22: Bolt

Chris lay on the concrete floor of his kennel in the dark, his eyes open.

There was a soft padding sound of footsteps. Chris remained still, staring at the wall. A metallic clink, and a scraping, the sound of a key carefully removed, but no other noise, no whine of the door opening.

Chris rolled partway over and saw Sad Face squatting there in the shadows. The man spoke in an urgent whisper: "It's almost a new moon and it's cloudy. This is the best chance we got. Slow count to five hundred after I go. Out of here, go left, and head straight for the tree line. You'll have to cross a wide-open section of the yard. Mind the fence at the tree line. About a half a kilometer in and there's a creek. Don't follow the driveway. Don't try to go another way. Go into the woods and follow the creek. It will take you west then south and meet the highway."

"What about the dogs?"

"I'll be with the dogs. Don't worry."

"Hey," whispered Chris, "what's your name, man?"

Sad Face's expression was unreadable in the darkness.

140

"Good luck, Chris."

***

Dark clouds hovered low over the towering conifers, roiling like slow-motion river rapids. Wind pushed the treetops and intermittent gusts swept down to bully the grasses and weeds.

Chris crept from the kennel building. Hunched, he ran to a discarded water tank and eyed the grassy expanse, granite gray in the darkness, between himself and the trees that hemmed the property.

He listened. Sounds of wind and dancing foliage filled his ears. He wondered where Sad Face had taken the dogs. Running naked through the forest he could do. Outrunning dogs that had his scent, and barefoot? That worried him. He wondered how long his co-conspirator could hold the others at bay. With luck, he'd have til morning and maybe that would be enough.

Chris ran for the tree line, moving as quickly as he dared for fear of unseen trash and scrap. A gashed foot or a broken ankle would spell disaster most likely.

Then, for some reason he could not fully grasp, he slowed, then stopped altogether. The wind dropped for just a second before roaring back into his ears but in that gap he... He stood a second longer, frozen like a deer.

Something wasn't right. Something about the tree line, the shadows. Some sound under the wind. He backed up, eyes on the property line some fifty yards away. He spun and trotted for the driveway. There were six vehicles, assorted trailers, and various parts arrayed there in a jumbled mess. Maybe he could find a vehicle with keys. Even if he was wrong about the trees, even if he was just succumbing to paranoia, it made a hell of a lot more sense to drive out of here than to hike through the woods with no shoes, naked as the day he was born, battered and bruised, to the highway and then... what? Ask a nice lady for a ride?

Chris should have asked his nameless helper for some spare boots. He should have-

The rustling of grass became a shuffling of bodies through brush behind him. He risked a glance over his shoulder. Shadow men and their shadow hounds poured from the darkness.

Chris was sprinting now. He had a considerable lead but he could not hope to outrun dogs on open ground. He hoped they had them on leashes.

He made the driveway, cut between two parked trucks, and dropped down, ducking around the front of one of the trucks to end up crouched between a cattle trailer and a van. He tried the van door. Locked. At any moment he expected to be bowled over by one of the dogs, hamstrung or torn open at the throat.

Consciously keeping his breathing under control, he scooted over to a pick-up and stood on tip-toes to look in, trying to spot keys left in the ignition. He tried the door. Locked.

The dogs were braying and barking now. They must be leashed or they would have had him by now.

"Spread out, he's in there. Get around all of it! Box him in."

"Get the fucking house lights on! House lights!"

Chris scouted visually for deeper shadows, brighter areas, trying to formulate a plan, trying to find a way out.

He climbed up onto the roof of the truck, then stretched across the gap to the roof of the van and laid down flat.

Booted feet crunched on gravel. They had reached the driveway. Flashlight beams roved, casting long shadows among the vehicles.

Off in the direction of the house, footfalls pounded hollowly up the front porch and the external lights flashed on, throwing a white glow over the driveway, casting expressionist shadows with the intersecting angles of the vehicles.

Directly beside the van came the Mustache Man with the Rottie on a leash. The dog leapt at the side of the van and barked.

"Got you, you little shit."

Chris sprang to his feet and leapt from the roof of the van, landing directly on the dog, feeling the crunch and snap of its body under his bare feet. When the dog had menaced him in the basement, it had seemed a powerful beast; when he feared pursuit from the unleashed dogs, they seemed impossible opponents. Now, feeling the animal smashed beneath him, hearing the strange, strangled whine, it felt so weak, like a delicate creature, a little thing of fine china.

There was no way Chris could keep his balance but he had forward momentum. As he landed he pushed forward, slamming the man back. The Mustache Man hit his head on the neighboring truck's passenger window.

Chris pushed off from him, staggered to the side, and made to leap between the truck and the trailer hitched behind it, but he caught his foot on the hitch rigging and spilled forward. The hitch knob banged painfully against his knee. He rolled and saw the Mustache Man on the other side of the obstacle.

144

"Come here, fucker," barked the Mustache Man.

The enemy lunged over the hitch, swinging his baton down. Chris kicked out at his chest and struck a glancing blow. The baton smashed down on his shin and he cried out. Mustache Man got hold of Chris's ankle and pulled. Chris kicked out repeatedly, grunting and yelling. Despite the herky-jerky battering of Chris's feet, the Mustache Man held fast to the leg and beat at it with his baton.

"Fucking animal! Get the fuck over here, you dumb fucks! Help me!"

Chris pulled his leg toward his chest and the Mustache Man stumbled forward, catching his knees on the hitch and losing his grip on Chris's leg.

Chris kicked out hard and connected with the other man's chest. Mustache Man grunted in pain. Desperate not to lose his window of opportunity, Chris grasped the fender and hauled himself to his feet. His leg hurt badly. He grabbed Mustache Man by the shirt and hauled him sloppily over the hitch. The struggling Mustache Man struck at Chris's flanks with the baton and both men spilled to the gravel.

Chris rolled to the dominant position, punched and grappled, slammed Mustache

145

Man's wrist to the ground and chopped at it, knocking the baton away. He got his hands on the throat, pressing, strangling, striking Mustache Man in the face and then strangling some more, bearing down with all the rage fueled strength he could summon.

Mustache Man kicked his legs and struck at Chris's head, flapping his arms like wings. His face went puffy, first red, then maroon. He twisted his hips. He pried at Chris's hands. Veins bulged on his forehead. Chris growled, veins bulging in his own face, his vision narrowing as blood pumped up his neck, his face showing the same reddening strain as that of his enemy.

A burning mist blasted Chris in the face. He felt like his eyeballs were melting. His nostrils burned, and he couldn't draw a breath. He fell back bellowing.

Mustache Man shouted in dismay, coughed, retched, convulsed, trying to roll away from the cloud of pepper spray.

Swift, sure footsteps crunched in the gravel. It was the man with the sad eyes, a look of wild, sweaty elation on his face. He held a broomstick, which he pressed into Chris's stomach. He kicked Chris in the shins and pressed the pole harder into his belly, the whole time grinning, panting, his eyes bugging out of his head.

Chris grabbed hold of the stick and pried it away from his gut. He rolled, curling himself into a protective fetal position. Sad Face pushed at Chris's shoulder, trying to roll him, but Chris resisted. Sad Face struck him about the legs and back with the broomstick and then pushed the cowering Chris over with a foot.

Through his gushing, stinging eyes, Chris caught a glimpse of the Truck Driver, with the remaining two dogs on leads, strolling in like he was taking his pets for an evening piss and some exercise.

Sad Face sat on Chris's chest and pressed the wooden pole lengthwise against his throat. Chris was nearly blind; his eyes and nose ran uncontrollably. Thick salty snot poured into his throat. Chris tried to open his eyes but couldn't bear that bug-eyed, joyous face, that eager, hungry look that stared back at him. He wrenched his head to the side.

Sad Face eased the pressure on the broomstick enough to grab Chris's face and turn it back up toward him.

"Look at me," he said. "Ha! Fucking dumb faggot."

He spat on Chris's face and began a grotesque parody of crying.

147

"Oh boo hoo hoo, you're aah awone. Nobody wuvs yew. Why the fuck would I help your gay ass? You know how much money I made off you? Ten grand. Ten fucking thousand dollars betting on you. Bitch! Ha ha! Fucking cry about it."

He maced Chris again, coughing and laughing in the cloud, his eyes now red and watering too.

Sad Face pressed his palm into Chris's face, smushing it and grinding the back of his head into the gravel. Chris pissed himself. Tears ran down his face.

The Driver decided that the sad-faced man had had enough fun.

"A'right, a'right, a'right. He fuckin' pissed himself. Get up off him, it's disgusting."

Sad Face rose, belted Chris on his bare ass with the broom handle with a final, resounding smack. He brandished the pole. "You're lucky I didn't ram this up your fucking ass." He made to jab it toward Chris's crotch. "Or pop your fucking balls with it," he cackled.

Mustache Man sat in the dirt, his face in his hands, moaning. The Driver and Sad Face raised Chris up between them. The Mustache Man stood with difficulty, wiping his eyes and blowing snot from his nose with a noise like a wet trumpet. He cursed.

Chris expected to be struck or verbally as-
saulted by the Mustache Man, but Mustache
spoke instead to Sad Face, his voice a hoarse
croak:

"Good job getting all that fucking mace in my
face, asshole."

"Aw did I get a little in your eye, baby?
What's the matter, I thought you like shots to
the face, faggot." Sad Face was still running in a
state of high sadistic arousal.

Chris clenched his eyes shut. Tears and snot
ran down his face.

***

In the dismal, wood-paneled cellar hallway,
the man with the mustache and the man with
the drooping face passed a joint between them.
A muffled din blasted against the door from inside the basement cell.

In his old cell, curled in the fetal position
on the cold concrete floor, Chris made more
noise than he had made in quite some time. The
Bluetooth speaker blasted at full, overwhelming volume – so loud the woofers crackled and
threatened to give out. It blasted the hoarse, col-
ic-stricken screaming of an infant. You could
hear the redness of its struggling, unseen little

face as it cried out over and over in a pain it had no words to express.

In the gaps between the infant's tortured cries, Chris cried out too, his voice similarly raw, broken, tormented by something so utterly beyond him, an indescribable bereavement. The infant and the man shrieked in hellish call and response.

All the while, Sad Face and the Mustache Man leaned against the wall outside, smoked together, and listened.

Chapter 23: Machine Dream III (Tractor)

Leering faces pressed close, contorted with prurient glee. The eyes were protruding bulbs. A sea of faces pressed together above reaching, clawing hands, pumping fists, a foaming ocean of blood lust.

Chris had always had a sense of paper thinness, the whole universe as a flat surface projected onto his eyeballs. A feeling that when he faced forward, he had no back, that the unseen was there but amorphous, undefined. It was why he smoked spliffs instead of joints: when he got too high, the feeling would be unbearable. Tobacco would tamper this melding of claustrophobia and vertigo and ground him in his body. He could go forward and not worry so much about the unseen; the fleeting tingle of nicotine through his limbs would give him a sense of thickness, of biological substance that fought the feeling of depthless, membranous semi-being he experienced even when sober.

He would feel sometimes, with people, that they were pressed right against his eyeballs, so close that reaching out to touch them was pointless. Seeing was contact and it was inescapable. No distance, just a one-dimensional press. This was why wild places appealed to him: if you're going to have something pressed to the screen of your being, why not that? Why not a mountain, the trees, the night sky, the murky wafting smoke of distant wildfires?

Now Chris felt the pressing weight of the images before him and felt himself forced backward through the membrane. Pushed far from what he knew into what was behind him and always had been. He soaked through the skin. What had once been an imminent visual pressure became a distant inversion of itself, removed by an unimaginable distance. Yet he was able to see it all as if through a microscope. Every pore and follicle, every stain on the teeth, every bead of sweat or flying drop of spittle. He saw it all but none of it could touch him.

It was beyond comprehension. Chris knew he was there, on the other side; no longer suffused and buried by the projection but remote from it, observing. In his body and outside of it all at once.

The final immersion.

The breach.

***

Bare feet gripping black asphalt. Chris faced

a fat man with a huge soft belly like an over-ripe fruit, cone-shaped breasts, a wild, un-kempt beard, and a shoulder-length puff of tan-gled curly hair. They brandished machetes. The fat man's shins and forearms were protected by crude armor made of wooden slats wrapped with twine like some primitive hockey goalie. Drums pounded. Or was it the beating of his own heart? Chris could feel his pulse in his neck, throbbing in time with the hollow, resonant sound.

A circle of tractors surrounded the tarmac arena, their engines pummeling a relentless ma-chine tattoo.

Wolves on distant hills disappeared, trotting away, becoming vanishing specks. Chris was under attack by dream dogs, bathed in head-lights. The wolves were too far to see clearly but he knew they had stopped and looked at him. He knew because distance was not real, they were not far away, their projections had merely shrunk on the membrane that surrounded him. He tried to keep his footing as the dogs latched one after another onto his arms, the weight in-creasing, becoming too great, dragging him down.

The burlap-draped hierophant with the big, lumpy head. A scarecrow-like idol. Dogs circled it, sniffing at the ground as if looking for something but who knew what? The Bobblehead made the Anubis hand sign with His left and held His right across His stumpy torso, palm pressed to where the heart should have been.

Chris's machete slashed the Fat Man's belly, splitting it like a tomato. The roar of the crowd, the roar of the tractors. White slimy fat oozed forth like yogurt from a tube.

Chris was sopping wet. He didn't know if it was sweat still on him from the hot car or water still on him from the pressure washers or blood still on him from Scrawny Ass and Blade Arms and Redbeard and...

The Fat Man was stumbling back, howling.

Spinning red fractals of dog heads in dog heads in dog heads...

Chris charged forward, gripped the fat neck, and pushed. The deafening percussive throb of the tractor engine loomed close, the drive belt spinning on a huge wheel on the exposed engine. Chris shoved the Fat Man's head back. The belt caught the hair. The Fat Man grimaced. Chris saw the plaque piled around his corroded gums. The fat hands pushed at Chris's pectorals, fighting for life.

Chris rammed the Fat Man's head and the back of the skull was ground to mush in the spinning, pounding machine parts. The roar of the tractor was deafening, the hooting crowd lost in the noise.

Blood and brain matter spattered Chris's face, got in his mouth.

"Drop it."

The trashed Fat Man fell to the tarmac.

The dream dogs ripped at his arms, leapt to snap at his throat.

Chris held a gory, sticky hammer. His feet felt loose dirt, not asphalt.

He pounded a head flat with the hammer.

"Drop it."

The hammer hit the dirt.

Chris sat cross-legged on the dirt. The dogs circled, they looked him in the eyes, they rushed for his throat but he did not flinch. They were ripe with the musky scent of wet canine, like they had just been swimming.

Chris slammed one man into another. Identical twins with white-blonde hair. He was using one, gravely wounded, as a riot shield to slam the other against a wall. Swirling red fractals like the open mouths of dogs, black and red gums, and in front of it, two ducks head to tail, spinning against each other, spinning spinning spinning...

One of the twins was dead on the ground. Chris stood over the other with a club in both hands raised high above his head.

"Drop it," said the Truck Driver.

He brought down the club, braining the twin. He heard laughter, a wheezing, squeaking noise like an old office chair.

"Drop it."

Chris threw the club to the dirt.

The dogs brought him down. His head hit the dirt. Roar of the crowd.

The bodies of the identical twins spun head-to-foot like the ducks, gore streaming from their pulverized faces to join the swirling fractal colors.

Chris's enemy wore paint on his body and face. Runes and geometric markings. The watching crowd had wooden faces, frozen in open-mouthed horror or wide-grinning manic glee or contorted snarls, eyes and mouths like knots in trees. They reached for Chris with metal hands and he feared his flesh being pinched and torn off by their hinges and joists.

He swung a hammer and caved in the chest of the Painted Man, who folded like a book. Chris did not see him flatten again, it was like he folded into singularity and was gone.

"Drop it."

A skinny man with no legs bounded along on his hands. Chris was unarmed, on the defensive.

156

He crawled toward a spear, stretching, reaching.

The Bobblehead towered over the BC interior like a plume of brown wildfire smoke. He rose and rose until His pillar of smoky being collided with the sky and spread, blanketing all that could be seen, blocking the sun. Spreading downward, suffusing all the air with foul sepia.

A broken spear stuck from the shoulder of the Legless Man as Chris grabbed his enemy by the hair and sawed at his throat with a dagger.

The crowd: men in masks with well-behaved dogs on leashes, sitting.

The head is separated from the body. From the neck stump, a volcano of disgusting fractals bloomed like dog-mouth flowers.

Chris stood with the severed head hanging by the hair before the blurry figure of the Bobblehead, who sat upon a throne, imperial, beatific, ethereal. A horrible Boschian figure. He sat with arms folded, hands hidden in rough-woven, sagging sleeves.

Dogs sat around His throne, others wandered and sniffed. Tessellated dog heads churned like the surface of the sun behind Him.

"Drop it," said the Bobblehead.

Chris tossed the head of the Legless Man toward the throne. The dogs came forth to sniff and lick at it. Some encircled Chris, sniffing at him. One of the dogs raised a leg and pissed on the head. Chris watched all of this, then looked to the enthroned figure.

"Good boy."

The Bobblehead opened His hands. Fractals poured forth.

Part IV

All Dogs Go To Heaven

Chapter 24: A Nice Home

A crashing like gunshots. Deafening, skull-smashing.

"Wakeupwakeupwakeup, wake up, little baby!"

Sad Face was smashing a metal pry bar against the door of Chris's kennel and shouting.

"C'mon c'mon c'mon c'mon, up up up upupu-pup."

At each word, the betrayer whacked the bars, *klang klang klang klang*, sending shocks through Chris's whole being, like he had a body of metal that resonated with each impact, the noise resounding through his hollow insides.

At a touch on the shoulder from the Truck Driver, Sad Face stepped back, and the Driver opened the cage.

"Come," said the Driver.

Chris came.

The courtyard was bright with the radioactive light of a round, red moon rendered chiaroscuro by the haze. The air smelled of charcoal. Chris looked at his feet.

As the Mustache Man closed in to put a bag on his head, Chris noticed the discoloration of bruises around the man's neck and felt... some-

160

thing. He didn't know what. A memory of pride perhaps, or something else. Words and feelings failed in his mind, fizzling on contact. But he looked for just a second before he was bagged and he felt whatever it was.

They put a white bag over his head instead of a black one, and he could still partially see through it in the bright moonlight. Like looking through gauze.

Chris walked with the men to the driveway and crawled into the truck box, onto the now-familiar ribbed surface of the metal floor. The tailgate slammed him into darkness. Before long, they were moving. Chris bounced with the motion of the vehicle.

***

The drive seemed longer than usual.

When the truck ground to a halt, the men left him lying in the dark box for some time. Chris felt the creak and slam of the driver and passenger doors of the truck. He heard soft, serious talking amongst the Driver and the Mustache Man. Then another voice, one he had never heard before, an elderly man's voice.

"You are late."

"We're moving dangerous cargo, it's compli-

161

cated-"

"You smell high and drunk."

There was silence for a while. The new voice came again, unintelligible but audibly stern.

The tailgate squeaked open and a shaft of dim light illuminated the white fabric over Chris's eyes.

"Come," said the Truck Driver.

Chris had no compunction to disobey. He shimmied on his back to the tailgate and slid down to the ground, feeling the cool pavement on his bare soles. He was seized then by the alien grip of unfamiliar hands. He heard breathing at his shoulder level and smelled a novel mixture of perfume and old man scent.

"We'll take him from here. You wait outside. If he dies, you're responsible for disposal."

The new handlers pulled him along. Chris could see a little through the hood: contours of cars streaked by reflected moonlight, a large house, silhouettes of trees and shrubbery. He heard tinkling streams of water falling into a pool. He felt a honeycomb of cobblestones underfoot, the occasional press of a pebble. Then he was in the full darkness of the shadow of the house and even his semi-transparent sack was enough to take what little vision he had.

Chris felt the caress of grass under his feet.

162

It was soft, fresh, not like the dry straw where he was kept. Then the gritty touch of cool cinder blocks. Under the ubiquitous smoke, he smelled flowers, freshly mowed lawn, fragrant trees, and cool water with a hint of chlorine.

As they rounded a bend, Chris could make out a rabble of noise but it was not the usual rough buzz of the blood-thirsty men at his matches. This was rough, certainly, but different. Presences nearby, other bodies, the sound of a gate opening smoothly. They pushed him under the deeper shadow of an archway. A moist, verdant scent bloomed in his nostrils, and the murmur of noise grew louder and clearer: the snarling of dogs, a tangle of savage animal sounds.

The light changed too: it got brighter. The red-gold light of the sick moon seemed to hit planet side and through the bag came the churning dance of flame and black shadow. Under the rabid yarl of the dogs was the crackle of fire. A black mass, a wall of people; in the gauze blur of the sack, they changed height and shape with the pulsing of the flames.

The dog sounds came closer, the crowd parted and Chris was pushed through. He felt a swoosh of air around his bare legs as the dogs passed within snapping distance.

163

He was pushed down to his knees. A palm pressed the top of his head, holding him in place as a knife cut diamond-shaped holes in the fabric in front of his eyes and he saw now with clarity.

He was in the immaculate, ornate garden of a large house, part of a densely packed circle of dozens of men and women in crude wooden dog masks of various breeds painted in vivid, unnatural colors - purples, greens, yellows, oranges...

The men wore robes of ruby red, the women sheer white through which their nude bodies could be seen. About their necks the women wore leather collars, with rings of thorns and flowers atop their masked heads. The men wore tiaras of splintered bone and necklaces of yellow and white teeth. Many of the women bore torches. Some of the men held the leashes of seated dogs that shifted and licked their lips nervously at the violence and tumult before them but remained obedient.

Above them hung the tangerine moon. In the middle of the circle two snarling pit bulls tore at each other.

Chris had little interest in the dog fight and looked instead around the circle of people. He couldn't tell if anyone was looking at him because of the masks; they seemed engrossed in the animal violence before them.

Directly across from him was another nude and white-hooded man on his knees, like a mirror image. He had no eyes for Chris and watched the dogs with rapt attention. His chest heaved. His penis was erect.

Chapter 25: Garden Party

When one dog had murdered the other, the audience applauded.

The victorious animal was gravely wounded and was clubbed out of its misery by a fat man in a crooked bulldog mask that seemed too small above his double chin, like a raft floating on a sea of face.

Chris felt an expectant pressure and looked up to see those nearest him staring down, eyes leering from behind grotesquely festive masks. He saw dilated pupils through round and almond-shaped eye slits.

Two unseen figures pulled him to his feet. A woman walked to him from one of the dog corpses. She wore a collie mask of purple and lime green with floppy ears woven of hair. She gripped his penis in a blood-coated palm, painting it cherry red, then drew a dog paw with dabs of blood on his chest, above the heart. Finally, she pressed her palm to his face, stamping the white linen with a dainty hand print. Directly across from him, The Other Man was being identically anointed.

Another woman threw a bunch of flower petals in Chris's face. It was all a little disorienting.

166

In the center of the circle, the Fat Bull dog Man held two swords in an X across his chest. The Collie Woman and the woman who had blessed the Other Man - in a beagle mask of white and chartreuse - each took one of the swords from Bulldog Man. The Collie Woman came to Chris and placed the weapon gingerly in his hands. The eyes behind her mask locked onto his.

The sword was a simple but beautiful thing: an unadorned bastard with a tapering three-and-a-half foot blade that seemed to twist and lash about, the way it reflected the swirling fire-light. The crossguard was a straight bar, the grip two-thirds brown leather, the lower half-hand of bare metal, narrowing toward a pommel in the likeness of a dog's head. It was surprisingly light in his hands.

The attendants drew back, widening the cir-cle so that Chris and the Other Man now stood inside the ring of onlookers. There was an ex-tended silence in which the only sounds were the crackling of torch flame, the tinkle of water, and the stirring of the shrubbery in the breeze.

Then the women knelt as a hunched and very elderly man in a magenta terrier mask with blades of grass for whiskers walked around the inside circumference of the circle, pouring small white rocks from a red sack to form a boundary between the spectators and the combatants. As he did this, the masked watchers began a snarling monotonous chant, punctuated by percussive barking noises and yips.

With slow steps to match the plodding hum of the pagan vocalization, a man walked to the center of the circle, trailed by two hound-faced women in sheer white swinging dog head thuribles on long gold chains, so low they swept just above the ground, snakes of incense shimmying up from the blood-flecked grass.

Dressed and masked differently from the other men, this man seemed to occupy some higher position, a man of office, a priest of whatever horrible religion these rites represented. He wore vermilion robes with gold trim and a black stole likewise trimmed in gold filigree. His dog mask was a black pit bull with a red patch around one eye and gold whiskers protruding from the wide snout. From the mouth hung a desiccated red flap like a piece of fruit leather; it seemed to Chris to be a real severed tongue. On his head was a tall mitre of ribs and leg bones, a papal crown of death. He made the Anubis head with his left hand and raised his right with two fingers pointing skyward.

"We offer this sacrifice to The Master," intoned the Pit Bull Priest with a grave ceremonial air. "As He hath willed: the victor and the vanquished. One cannot rise but to climb a mountain of slain enemies. And so we shall pile our Lessers beneath us and rise and to Him offer divine triumph and divine destruction. His power shall be mine."

A chorus of male voices echoed, "His power shall be mine."

The Priest turned to face the Other Man square-on, then turned one hundred eighty degrees to face Chris. Finally, with arms upraised, he turned a full three-sixty, the incense women each doing a full lap around him, after which, his duties done, he let his arms fall with nonchalance and retreated to join the circle of voyeurs.

A dissonant gong clanged.

Chris knew what was expected of him. He raised his sword up into what forgotten movies had told him was a reasonable guard position. The two men closed in on each other in silence, circling. The Other Man's tumescent, bloody cock wagged with each step.

The crude holes in the hood obstructed Chris's peripheral vision and he worried that the fabric would twist or pull back, blinding him. He watched his opponent's eyes, alert for twitches, hints of an attack.

169

The Other Man made probing swings and jabs at Chris, too far away yet to be a real danger, testing Chris's responses. Chris lashed out with a low sweep for the thighs. The Other danced back and parried.

The onlookers were indistinct to Chris, a flat backdrop of white, red, and a smear of other colors from which his designated enemy stood out stark and clear, the only real object in a melting projection.

The Other Man barked and charged in. He brandished his sword high and made to slash downward but this proved to be a feint and at the last moment he thrust his blade for Chris's abdomen. Chris was fooled; his parry was too big, intended to block a high arcing slash. Only barely was he able to correct the motion and bring his sword down to block in time. The blades scraped to the ricasso. The parry knocked the attacker's stabbing point aside but the cutting edge ran along Chris's left side and sliced a long gash. Hot blood trickled down to his thigh.

Chris jumped to the right and pushed against the enemy blade, but he overbalanced and almost tripped. The Other Man pressed in after him with a swift and decisive horizontal swing aimed at the neck. Chris ducked under the strike, lost his footing, and slashed out, his sword in his left, his right going out as a counterweight. He fell but the swing connected, slicing his opponent across both thighs, coming within millimeters of the Other Man's scrotum. Chris tumbled to the soft grass and rolled.

The Other's next attack came a fraction of a second too late, just missing Chris's wrist as he somersaulted away. He felt the swoosh of air as the blade threatened to sever his hand.

The Other was now open in the aftermath of his wide swing. In one motion, Chris rolled to his feet and sprang at the Other Man, butting his head and shoulder into the hooded man's hard abdomen. He wrapped his arms around his opponent, so when they fell, the Other landed on the flat of Chris's sword. Chris had the dominant position, but his arm was pinned beneath the hot, muscled back. With his free hand, he pressed the enemy's sword arm to the ground.

Chris tried to knee him in the crotch but could only hit the thigh and glute. He pressed his forehead against the Other's face and tried to push the fabric of the enemy's hood, twisting the eye holes out of place. He succeeded in this, blinding his opponent, but in the process, he pushed his own eye holes askew and had only a partial field of vision.

Growling his frustration, the Other Man

171

twisted and bucked, trying to throw him. Chris held fast to the enemy's wrist and in the awkward contorting that ensued bashed the hand against the ground, knocking the sword hilt free. Chris grabbed it, jerked his pinned arm out, abandoning his own sword beneath the enemy, rolled away, and somersaulted to his feet. He stumbled backward, fighting to establish his balance. Chris held the sword one-handed in his left and shook his almost-numb right hand.

The Other Man pushed to a sitting position and scrambled for Chris's discarded weapon pinned between the grass and his own buttocks but Chris was already charging in with the Man's own weapon. He swung down one-handed and scored the enemy's shoulder, splitting the collarbone with the mid-blade. The Other Man howled.

Chris took the hilt in a two-handed grip and yanked the blade free, spattering his legs and crotch with hot blood. Before the Other Man could fall back from his seated position, Chris swept his blade horizontally.

The head was severed from the body, hit the grass, and rolled toward the edge of the circle, stopping just short of the ring of white stones. The hood slipped from the head in its tumble and Chris saw the face of a man like any oth-

172

er, nothing remarkable save a haggard, ragged beard not unlike his own.

The body fell back heavily, squirting blood from the neck stump as the heart pumped its final beats.

Chris staggered back a few steps and cast the gore-coated bastard sword to the turf. The hood stuck to his face, pasted with sweat.

A soft patter of applause. No jeering, no hooting, no ruckus at all. Not a word spoken. Just a gentle titter of golf claps.

The Collie and Beagle Women approached. The Collie Woman reached to peel the hood from Chris's face, then the Beagle draped a garland of flowers about his neck.

Chris gazed about, slack-jawed and panting. The air felt cool on his face after the confines of the hood.

Two other women bent near the body of the slain Other, one rising with Chris's victorious sword in hand, the other with the head. Falling to their knees and bowing low, they presented these items to the Pit Priest, who took up sword and head in turn and held each aloft as he walked a slow lap, displaying the prizes to the appreciative audience.

The ring of onlookers closed in like zombies, some reaching out to caress Chris's chest and arms. Lustful fingers probed at the wound in his side, coming away blood-coated and causing Chris to cringe with pain.

The Collie Woman and the Beagle Woman each clasped one of Chris's hands and led him through a gauntlet of nodding, clapping masked figures. Everywhere he looked he met hungry eyes peeping through round holes and narrow slits.

The Pit bull Priest came to walk before Chris, parting the crowd while holding the dripping head and wet, viscera-painted sword high. The incense women flanked him, swirling their dangling gilded dog heads. Smoke billowed from the eyes and mouths of the metal heads to swirl about the ankles of Chris and his escorts, the weird perfume rising and writhing on the breeze to join the haze that stained the sky.

With the Priest as their gruesome parade master, the throng pushed Chris like a river current along a winding path of trimmed hedges and sweet flowers to a wide portico of faux classical columns adorned with cherubs and wreaths.

At a set of wide patio doors, the Priest stepped to one side, and through the holes of the pit bull mask, Chris saw brown eyes creased by smile lines.

"Congratulations," said the Priest.

Then the women took him through the back door.

***

Past the threshold the applause grew muffled and finally died.

They took him to the second floor, then along a hall to a door the reddish-pink hue of stained cedar. It had a die-cast knob in the shape of the head of a snarling dog.

"Open it," said the Collie Woman. Despite her face covering, Chris could tell that she smiled. Her voice was eager, almost breathless. "Go ahead."

Chris looked from the Collie Woman to the door to the other dog woman. Their eyes were wide and blandly manic like the evangelical housewives he used to see alongside preacher husbands on Sunday morning TV. When he reached for the knob their eyes followed his hand and then darted back up to his face to lock eyes with him. He turned the knob.

His ears pulsed and throbbed. Blood and salt burned his eyes. The insides of the Other Man were all over him. He felt a swimming emptiness.

The door swung silently inward.

Chris was falling, spinning, in a brown abyss that pressed in from all sides as though he were drowning in gelatin.

Chapter 26: Contract Negotiation

"Hello."

Chris's vision was a red-brown smear. He thought he was still plunging into the abysmal jelly, but as the vision resolved he saw subtle pencil delineations that became woodgrain and realized his eyes were hypnotically glued to the floor. Still dizzy, he followed the warping lines to a burgundy carpet, on which sat a low chair of umber leather and ornately carved limbs. Beyond that, a wide wooden desk stained like a tiger's eye.

The door behind him was shut, though he had no memory of hearing it close or of doing so himself.

"Please have a seat."

He knew that voice. The dribble of the vowels, the wet smack of lips on the consonants, the throaty bass rumble behind it all.

Chris's feet peeled from the hardwood, every nuance of sticky sound cutting through the death-like silence. Blood still ran from his hip and down his leg to leave red stamps of pad prints on the floorboards.

He sat himself in the armchair.

"Welcome."

177

The Bobblehead sat behind the desk, draped in His burlap robe and cassock like a decrepit pope. He wore a garland of red and white roses and a necklace of human molars and canine fangs that had rotted to the color of cider. To Chris the being seemed to strobe between states, one second looking like a human male wearing the skinned face of a dog, the next flickering second like a real dog-man hybrid, a monster with an almost comically large slobbering pit bull head atop a stunted humanoid form. It seemed to slide and glitch between these two states: gross mask of dog-leather and otherworldly beast.

The dog-headed man did not look at Chris but looked at a top carved from yellow-gray stone that He fingered on the desk, holding it poised and turning it idly with leathery, clawed hands. He spun it with a twist of thumb and forefinger and the top became an ecru blur, whirring in a circle on the desktop with a sound like a scraping pencil on paper.

"Tops are born," said the Bobblehead. "They live..."

The top began to wobble, its pointed tip spinning out wider from its center until the sides touched the desk and the object was no longer spinning on point but rolling about, slowed by increasing friction.

"And they die," finished the Bobblehead. He flicked the dying top off the desk with a finger, then looked up at Chris. "Congratulations on your victory."

Chris met those golden yellow eyes. The face was clearer than he had ever seen it: black lips wet with slobber framing a comically wide mouth, thick black whiskers stabbing out from loose jowls, a charcoal stub of a nose, the wide-set eyes like jewels beneath the heavy brow, the thick, flat cranium, and clipped pointed ears. "How do you feel?"

Chris's lips were painfully chapped, his body crusted with gore. His mouth felt glued shut with thirst. His throat was scratched raw by the ever-present smoke in the air.

Behind the Bobblehead was a vertigo-inducing slip of red, dog-mouth fractals, black gums, and pink flesh. Tan teeth, ribbed textures of mouth-palate, churning with no depth like paper cutouts...

"How do you feel?"

Chris's voice was a thin rasp, brittle as peeling paint. "Fine."

"You should be proud. I was watching. You have done well. Do you like your trophy?"

The creature gestured at the desktop, where

the sword-length prosthesis Chris had amputated from Blade Arms in the chain link octagon days, maybe weeks or months ago lay like a great fountain pen.

"It is yours to keep."

Chris stared at the sword arm, transfixed. Finally, he broke away and met the eyes of the dog man, which now seemed more green than golden. Strings of goo hung on black lips.

"Do I take it and go?" Chris asked.

The Bobblehead laughed for a long time. "I have enjoyed you immensely, and my enjoyment does not end."

Those brown leathery hands rose to tent themselves below the chin, a thoughtful and delicate gesture that seemed absurd performed by such a crude parody of a being.

"Please," the Bobblehead said, "Consider what I say now: tonight was your first true victory. Your prize is opportunity." Here the creature paused, folding its hands once more on the desk. "Think of your past as training, a preparation for what comes next. Now you are a free agent, released from all ties, free to explore your options and accept offers. As it happens, I have an offer for you."

The Bobblehead pulled open a drawer that Chris could not see and brought forth a pen and a sheaf of paper, a neat stack of unbleached eggshell sheets with raw edges. A clawed hand with skin the texture of an aged leather brief-case pushed the paper toward Chris's side of the desk. He placed the pen gingerly beside it. Pointed nails ticked against the desktop.

"You have shown tremendous promise throughout your training camp. I hoped that you would make it. How wonderful to see you here now, strong and safe. You have endured much without reward and I know it has been hard for you. But I am not the men you have known. I am different, as you see." The Bobblehead gestured vaguely to himself then continued. "I offer you rewards. Sign with me, and I will raise your career—already impressive for an amateur, I promise you—to new heights, and reward you accordingly. Austerity has made you strong. Now I promise you comfort, delicious food, females... Do you remember their particular pleasures? They are just outside. I would so like to breed you. You would make powerful sons and compliant daughters."

Chris's eyes strayed from the dog man's strangely human eyes and baggy visage to the sheet, dense with text.

"You may peruse it first if you wish," said the Bobblehead. "I will not be offended."

181

Chris scooched forward in his seat. The paper was more ink than beige space. He looked at his own naked legs. Crusted brown and dirt tangled his leg hair into knots. Away from the smoke and incense, he could smell the metallic taint of blood that clung to his body.

So long had it been since he'd known the simple dignity of clothing that he barely noticed his own nakedness anymore. But sitting before this being, this creature, made him feel exposed and vulnerable, even embarrassed, with an acuteness he had not felt since those earliest days in the basement, his first match in the pig barn... He saw his red penis and felt a surge of disgust.

With a great effort, Chris rose from his chair. He felt like a toddler, new to standing by his own power. He took a step toward the desk.

"That's a boy," said the Bobblehead.

Instead of the pen, Chris picked up the severed blade arm. He felt the cold, hairy flesh and the leather still wrapping it in a grid of straps and small buckles, felt the heft of the dirty blade.

In one great motion, Chris raised the bladed stump above his head like a scimitar, and with all the strength he could summon, he brought it down. The Bobblehead seemed to tilt His ugly face up to meet the descending blade. He made no move to block or evade as Chris swung. Instead, the man-creature began to laugh, a gurgling, wheezing rumble.

Chris split the giant cartoon head down the middle. The thickness of that bulldog skull sent a painful vibration through the dead arm into Chris's wrists and forearms. Under the force of the impact the Bobblehead's corpse bounced in its office chair as if shaking with hysterical enjoyment, the squeaking of the chair taking over where the throaty chuckle had stopped.

It took Chris a few mighty tugs to pull the blade from the vice of cloven bone. He leaned awkwardly across the large surface of the desk. The body rocked obscenely as he tugged, the chair creaking as if the Bobblehead teased and toyed with him, mocked him. The blade came free with a slurping sound and the body slumped forward onto the desktop, black ooze pouring from the split head like spilled ink.

Reality seemed to slip and glitch. Chris swayed where he stood, cradling his strange weapon, then turned and lurched for the door.

The rhythmic squeaking of the chair filled his ears like wheezing laughter.

183

Chapter 27: Free Agent

Chris pulled the office door open and stepped into the hall, swinging his grotesque sword to cleave the Beagle Woman through the collarbone. He pressed a foot to her stomach and pushed her from the blade. She slammed back against the far wall and slid to the floor, leaving a trail of dark blood. The Collie Woman was weirdly blank, watching this killing like a statue. When Chris turned to face her, his chest rising and falling in deep, steady breaths, she spun about and took off at a dead run down the hall.

He gave chase. She stumbled on the hem of her gossamer gown and he closed the distance in bounding strides. The floral crown she wore fell from her head. He raised the horrible arm above his head as he ran.

She had managed not to fall, hiked up her robe, and staggered, trying to recover her lost speed, but he caught up with her. With a gap of several feet still between them, he slashed, catching the fleeing woman with the tip of the blade, tracing a shallow gash down her back. She fell forward, tumbling down the stairs.

Chris leaped down after her. He took the stairs two at a time, trampling the woman

184

sprawled at the bottom. Her mask had fallen from her face. He stepped out into a wide stance. She was panting, moaning, trying to crawl away. He plunged the sword down through her brain stem, pinning her to the floor like a butterfly in a display case.

He tore the sword free.

Glitching. Reality melting. Chris could hear a noise like droning bass voices and throaty growling, crackling with electricity, from the belly of the house.

He followed the sound like a homing beacon around the balustrade to the basement stairs. These he descended calmly. At the end of a long corridor in the basement was a set of double doors, wide as the hallway. The portal seemed to float toward him, so mindless, so effortless was his approach.

Chris parted the panels of rich dark wood and looked in on a large and luxurious room festooned with lush rugs, cushions, and couches in various shades of red. On walls, shelves and tables were images and carvings of bestiality and dogs devouring women.

A fire burned in a wide brick fireplace. Along the mantle were sculptures of dog parts: disembodied heads, tails, legs, and paws in marble of fabulous jewel tones.

At the far end of the room the severed head of the Other Man oozed atop an ornate brazen plinth surrounded by candles.

Chris saw old men in various states of undress, some still in their ceremonial robes, others in boxer shorts or briefs. Most were nude. All still wore their masks. Some copulated with the women, others watched and masturbated, many toyed with flaccid penises. Their hair varied from white to salt-and-pepper to badly dyed black and brown. Many were balding. Paunches, varicose veins, awkwardly hiked-up dress socks on pasty legs. Some hirsute, others nearly as hairless as infants.

Most of the women were young. Most still wore their masks, though some had removed them to perform oral sex on pitiful and disgusting dicks.

Chris was looking for his special trio, the Truck Driver and his cronies. They were nowhere to be seen. Chris wondered where they were. Outside probably, smoking by the Ram, excluded from all this.

In the center of the room was a nude woman on all fours on an ottoman, copulating with a German Shepherd. She wore a Dalmatian mask of periwinkle blue with navy spots. By her head stood the Pit bull Priest, naked but for his necklace of teeth, mask, and pontifical bone crown. He raised Chris's victorious bastard sword high, poised for an executioner's descent, his eyes closed in ecstasy, mumbling some blasphemous prayer.

A harsh roar crescendoed in Chris's throat. Gripped by an unspeakable rage, he swung the severed arm blade about the room, not aiming, just swinging wildly, not caring whether he was killing or maiming or missing, just flailing and thrusting. Hitting people and furniture. Hitting lamps. Hitting sconces and trim. Hitting art objects. Splitting limbs and faces and torsos with his hideous weapon. Warm blood flecked his chest and face.

The room erupted into chaos. The zoophilic orgiasts screamed and scattered about, tripping over furniture and cushions and each other, tangling themselves in whatever remnants of ceremonial garb they still wore.

"Get the dogs! Get the dogs!"

"The dogs! The dogs!"

"*Fuck* the dogs, get a gun!"

Chris tackled a nude septuagenarian, slamming him to the ground and stabbing him through the mouth with the blade. Already Chris was soaked in fresh blood, new layers atop the old crusted brown.

187

He was beset by the horny shepherd, which growled and snapped at him. He used the arm to fend it off then kicked it hard in the ribs. Driven away, the dog gave up attacking Chris, turning instead on its master, made mad by the pandemonium around it. Snarling ferociously, its red erection waggling, it latched onto the leg of the Priest, who cursed and fell to the floor, dropping the ceremonial sword and striking the sex-slave dog about the head with impotent fists. He cried out for help from his fellows. A woman in a rottweiler mask tried to pull the furious animal off her Priest but the dog turned on her, taking her down by the throat. Her guttural scream became a hideous gargling that was finally silenced under the hysterical dog's attack.

A man with a doughnut-shaped salt-and-pepper goatee flailed about the room in a clueless panic, his erection bouncing. Chris swung the arm-sword at him. The man tried to leap out of the way but the sharp edge sliced cleanly through his penis. The man shrieked but was silenced when Chris ran him through.

Using the impaled man as a bulldozer, Chris shoved his way deeper into the panicking crowd, knocking people aside and impaling a second man. He slammed the two stacked bodies against the back of a sofa. As they tumbled onto the cushions, he wrenched his blade free.

Chris was hell-bent on the retrieval of his gladiator sword. He hacked and slashed with every step. He kicked men and women alike in the crotch and the belly, sending them flailing backward over couches. He punched faces and pulled fistfuls of hair.

He body-checked a robed man and sent the hedonist careening into the fireplace. The man thrashed and screamed, rolled from the flames, setting tapestry fringes and furniture alight, grabbing hold of one of the women in his mania.

Deafening gunshots rang out, impacting the floor and the furniture, causing an intensified surge of screaming from the cultists. The dog yipped with pain. A bullet struck a man Chris was stabbing, a dangerous near-miss that caused Chris to drop to the floor and roll behind the cover of a divan.

The floor in his hiding place was slick, the rug coated with blood. He looked up and found himself face to face with his vanquished enemy, the severed head of the Other Man gaping down at him from the plinth.

More shots and a whimper told of the fall of the renegade shepherd.

Chris turned and peered out over the divan like a wild predator hiding in tall grass, scanning the room, trying to spot the shooter in the rabble of bodies. The gunman was in a panic, he'd been firing willy-nilly and the gun now clicked empty.

"Fuck, fuck, *fuck!*" cried the shooter, fumbling to reload his pistol.

Chris leaped up with a cry and lunged for the plinth, grabbed a handful of the Other Man's hair, spun about, and threw the head overhand at the gunman. The head spun through the air trailing streamers of gore.

Skull hit skull with a sickening crunch. Pulverized teeth flew from the gunman's mouth. He tumbled backward, falling atop the maimed bodies of his fellows and their slave women.

Chris felt the heat of the spreading fire. He scanned the now nearly empty room. Cultists had poured out the double doors, down the hall and up the stairs.

A wounded woman buried herself under cushions in a corner. Chris plunged the blade arm into the pillows and left it standing there.

Nude bodies lay about like smashed slugs; robed corpses like discarded tissues from a nosebleed.

The Pit bull Priest crawled for the door, his mitre and mask abandoned, trailing blood and dragging his dog-mutilated leg, clinging to the bastard sword.

Chris crossed the room and slammed a foot down on the Priest's wounded calf, eliciting an agonized groan. He reclaimed the sword from the naked heathen, a weapon of both himself and his one-time enemy. He straddled the Priest and plunged the point into the spine between the shoulder blades. The clergyman gasped and fell limp. A maroon pool spread beneath him.

***

Emerging onto the ground floor, Chris heard a muffled pandemonium outside: shouting, gunshots, dogs going berserk, barking like mad, more gunshots, dogs whining and yipping. He heard the Mustache Man's enraged profanity quite distinctly, and the lower, less distinct rumbling shouts of the Truck Driver blending with the sound of motor vehicles.

In Chris's left hand hung the sword, in his right, dangling by the beard, the battered head of his vanquished colleague, the Other Man. One of the eyes had popped out on impact with the gunman; it hung by strings of muscle and nerve, dripping vitreous fluid, threatening to plop out at any second.

Rounding a corner, Chris startled a nude

woman who was crouched between a tall, mottled green vase and a potted fern. The Blue Dalmatian woman. Her eyes were wide behind her dog mask. She sprang to her feet and made for the kitchen. Her hips and back were scored by claw marks and her right arm hung limp and terribly mutilated, whether by himself or the berserk German Shepherd, Chris did not know. She favored her right leg as she ran, and she left a bloody footprint after each step.

He threw the decapitated head at her, hitting her on the back of her skull with a sound like two coconuts colliding. The Other Man's loose eye flew from the socket to splat against the wall.

The Blue Dalmatian stumbled forward, moaning in dismay, but managed to stay on her feet. She put the kitchen island between them and threw items at him, whatever she could grab: a cutting board flew wide and hit the door frame; a mortar hit his abs. She panted, backing away with increasing desperation as he circled. She pulled a butcher knife from a block.

Chris picked up the decapitated head and threw it. She ducked. The severed head sailed over her, trailing ribbons of gore, and smashed into an electric blender on the counter behind her, shattering both the glass container and its own bones. The woman screamed and brandished the knife.

Chris charged around the island at full speed, slashing with his sword to knock the knife from her hands. He grabbed her by the hair and ran his sword through her breast.

He let the body slump to the floor. From the counter he grabbed the now unrecognizingly disfigured head with bits of glass protruding from its flesh. The hair Chris used as a handle was attached by a torn flap of scalp. Blood and brain fluids gushed from the neck. Bits of shattered cranium and glass pattered against floor tiles.

Practically strutting, Chris headed for the front door. The sounds of terror outside had grown quiet.

***

Chris stepped out onto the front porch and was hit–*BAP!*–by a bullet in his right arm. The slug bit into the dog bite scar just below the crook of his elbow and stopped against the bone. The sword and the head dropped from his grip. He did a pirouette and hit the deck. His wounded arm sizzled with icy heat and the hand became a numb claw.

"Whoo!" came the exultant cry of the Mustache Man, the voice tiny with distance. "Gotcha, bitch!"

Chris lay beside a dead man whose throat and face had been torn away, and a pit bull full of seeping bullet holes. The wide salmon tongue lolled from the beast's mouth. He made eye contact with the animal's gold-flecked eyes. There was life in it, its ribs rising and falling with labored breath.

Chris's wounds leaked steadily, staining the veranda.

A small, feeble male voice, closer to the porch called out, "Is he dead?"

"Fuckin' got his ass," boasted the Mustache Man.

Chris gritted his teeth like a chimpanzee but he felt no anger; he was blank to the point of serenity, an emptiness as close to clarity as ever he had felt. He had come close to this feeling before, working away at his camp, preparing his meals, and hiking rough terrain with his rucksack. Now he lay with teeth bared in a grin of simian aggression, devoid of thought, a grim Buddha of violence.

He sprang up, snatched his sword, and sprinted to the side rail of the porch. More gunshots popped but he felt no new injuries, did not

194

flinch, and jumped the railing like a show dog on an obstacle course, his right arm hanging dead, swinging like a pennant. He bolted around the corner of the house.

Clear now from the immediate threat of gunfire, he forgot it completely; he was a being of the moment. He felt no fear, only presence, a wordless purpose that he knew with absoluteness. His focus turned from flight to attack, as if he had been in that state all along. He had no past and felt no fear of what was to come. He charged ahead like a furious automaton, powered by a thoughtless, relentless determination, guided by instinct alone, an inborn, physiological sense of purpose.

A middle-aged man, naked as the day he was born, scurried from under a shrub like a silverfish fleeing from a switched-on light bulb. He bolted in a lopsided and awkward run. His buttocks, flat as pancakes but still riddled with cellulite, jiggled like jelly. His pill-induced erection bounced, refusing to die down.

Chris intercepted, hacking him down forever. Then the pang of pursuing gunfire drove him through a vine-covered lattice archway into the garden.

195

Chapter 28: Fight/Flight

Storming the garden, his sword aloft, Chris scattered a dozen cultists like a child charging a flock of seagulls at the beach.

He intercepted a naked man in a red and pink pug mask with a protruding belly. Chris lobbed down with his sword. The Pug Man leaped back to evade and Chris's blade sliced cleanly downward through his potbelly, lopping it off. The thick hemisphere of flesh fell away. The Pug Man's eyes went wide and he drew a hissing gasp as his guts spilled forth, his intestines unfurling and piling onto the ground with wet plops. The fat man staggered backward and collapsed.

Chris ran on, trampling the soft plate of belly flesh that flattened beneath his foot like a pancake.

A robed, unmasked man climbed clumsily over a hedge. His draping garb tangled in the branches, and he twisted and jerked. Chris stabbed him through the neck.

Jostling cultists pushed through the archway. Like a herding dog, Chris drove them from the garden.

He came around to the driveway, which he

196

saw now was a tessellation of interlocking mandalas and spirals radiating from the central fountain. At the center of the fountain was a tri-leafed statue: a headless man peeing a stream of water; a rearing, headless dog doing the same; and a headless, armless female torso from which twin streams arched from the nipples.

Chris plunged into the midst of the parked cars clustered in the driveway, rampaging through a vehicular labyrinth. Panicked cultists dove into luxury cars, backing over others who cowered in the shadows underneath their vehicles. Chris moved through, killing those who fumbled with keys. He bent to stab and slash at men and women who cowered beneath the cars.

He tried the door of an occupied black sedan but the naked man inside had locked it. Throwing down his sword without a care, Chris pulled a shouting, struggling man by the legs from under the car. He struck the man about the face, then took him by the arm, swinging him about, sending the cowardly hedonist crashing face-first into the driver-side window of the locked car. The glass cracked and the occupant yelled in fear.

Chris heaved his Battering Ram Man, dazed and bloodied, and smashed the head once more into the spider webbed, red-smeared window.

The glass broke, knocking shards all over the occupant and gashing the face of Chris's living weapon. He pulled the Battering Ram Man from the broken window and threw him aside. The driver tried to crawl to the far end of the interior. Chris took up his sword and leaned in through the window, cutting his belly on glass shards. The man kicked in blind panic as Chris's sword stabbed at him, penetrating first the legs and then the torso.

Luxury vehicles driven by terrorized drivers crashed into each other like bumper cars.

Gunshots burst forth. The rear window next to Chris blew apart. The Truck Driver, the Mustache Man, and Sad Face, hanging far on the edge of things, had spotted Chris and opened fire, hitting pagans in their vehicles, hitting the wounded and the dead.

Chris crawled through the window, over the maimed body inside, popped the passenger door, and slid out. He dipped low, making off in a running crouch, serpentine through the vehicles.

"In, in, in! Surround him and get in there, close him in!"

The three men spread around and moved cautiously into the cluster of cars and carnage. Chris ran between two silver coupes and came under fire as Mustache Man popped around

198

the rear of a Porsche Cayenne. A window above Chris imploded.

Chris zigzagged through the maze, cutting his soles on bits of glass. He circled the tinkling fountain and came out onto the lawn, where he rose to his full height and sprinted off around the corner of the house.

"Go!" called the Truck Driver. "You, that way, you with me."

The gang split off, the Mustache Man after Chris, the Driver and Sad Face running in the opposite direction to head him off on the far side of the mansion, like children playing tag.

Thick smoke billowed from the windows. The smell of combustion was heavy in the air.

Chris ran through the garden archway and pressed himself back against the hedge. Mustache Man crept in, a Browning rifle poised against his shoulder. Chris leaped out and knocked the barrel aside with his sword. A round burst from the snout into the turf as Chris stabbed his tormentor through the belly. Mustache Man gasped, dropped the rifle, and fell to his knees. Chris pulled his sword free. Dark blood coursed from Mustache Man's guts.

Chris plunged his sword into the lawn. It stood like a crucifix. He picked up the rifle by the barrel. The metal burned his hand but he was unmoved and wielded the firearm like a club.

Mustache Man loped backward in a pained crab walk, a hand pressed to his abdomen to protect his stab wound. Chris advanced. Mustache Man collapsed, awkwardly supine, wincing in pain.

"Fuckin' animal," wheezed the Mustache Man.

Chris brought the rifle butt down with brutal force. The adversary was knocked flat, his nose broken.

Mustache Man hocked out thick, dark blood. He looked up at Chris with smoldering eyes, the mustache down-turned over a disgusted grimace.

"Fuck you, faggot," spat the Mustache Man.

Chris bashed him with relentless fury, wrecking teeth and jaw, cracking eye sockets. The cruel man gasped a few wet breaths, twisted, and kicked his legs.

When the face was raw hamburger and the torturer moved no more, Chris caught his breath a moment. He threw the rifle down on the corpse, unsheathed his sword from the turf, and jogged back the way he had come.

***

200

An ashen pillar billowed from the house, climbing ever higher, occluding the red moon and spreading to mingle with its wildfire-born brethren. The burning wilderness and the burning home united in the heavens.

Someone was driving over corpses to escape, dragging a body whose robes were tangled in the axle. Red smears went in all directions. Tire tracks streaked through the burst corpse of a rottweiler.

A severely wounded man crawled on the cobblestones amid the crushed corpses. Chris stabbed him dead and trotted along, wounded arm to his chest.

Stepping over dead dogs and trodding on human corpses, he mounted the porch. He paused to scoop up the head of the Other Man and entered the house.

***

Smoke detectors trilled incessantly. The floor was hot under Chris's feet. Smoke stung his eyes.

Sad Face leaped from a darkened doorway, swinging a heavy ax. Chris leapt aside and parried. The sword and ax blade met with a grinding friction. Sad Face's attack was waylaid only partly; the cutting edge bit Chris's thigh. The crossbar caught the curve of the ax blade and the two men struggled. Chris mashed the ruin of the Other Man's head into the morose visage of his enemy, eliciting a grunt of disgust.

Sad Face kicked Chris in the crotch. Chris dropped the head, stumbled backward, and fell on his ass. Sad Face spat the Other Man's fluid.

The ax wielder charged in, raising his weapon high and cutting down with mighty force. Chris brought his sword to bear, deflecting the blow, but the force of impact broke the sword just above the ricasso. A shock of pain ran through Chris's left arm. The sharp length of the blade flew away.

The deflection threw Sad Face off balance. Chris tossed his ruined weapon aside and threw himself forward, grabbing the traitor at the knees. Sad Face was bowled to the floor and Chris climbed on top of him, struck him in his pitiful face, and seized the ax by its long wooden handle, wrenching it from the enemy's grip. He clubbed Sad Face with the blunt end of the blade, tearing the flesh off his cheekbone.

Chris rose to his feet and stomped on the sad man's chest, pinning him flat. Sad Face grabbed for Chris's ankle. Chris kicked the grasping hand aside and swung the ax down, severing the hand from the wrist. Sad Face cried out in shock. Gouts of blood poured from the stump.

Chris pressed his foot into the solar plexus, holding the cruel man against the floor. Sad Face kicked his legs up, trying in vain to buckle Chris's knees. Chris swung the ax like a croquet mallet, burying it with a wet thud in his enemy's taint, obliterating his genitals. Blood soaked through the jeans. Sad Face squealed.

Using his foot to hold the thrashing Sad Face, Chris twisted the blade about, mutilating the crotch. Then he stepped on the sad man's throat, pressing down harder as Sad Face turned puce. Pleading eyes bugged out under the perpetually down-turned brows, becoming more and more distraught. Chris ground his heel.

Smoke was pouring up from the basement. Chris's eyes stung and tears ran down his cheeks. He lifted his foot and stepped back.

Sad Face coughed and sputtered, looked up at Chris with that pitiful gaze, and raised his remaining hand in a supplicating gesture.

"Please, man."

Chris stood panting. His eyes grew wide, whites visible all around. Sad Face held eye contact.

"Man," breathed Chris. His mind was flooded by the wordless memories of the false hope that this man had given him. Months of false kindness followed by unbearable grief and humiliation at the nightmarish realization that it was all the cruelest of games, the sick pleasure of a pure and malevolent sadist. A tumor of nauseous fury welled in his chest. He raised the ax over his head.

"MMAAAAAAAANNN!" screamed Chris. He swung the blade down, burying it with bone-crushing force in the center of the pathetic face that he loathed beyond imagining.

Sad Face's head slammed against the floor. The blade bit deep. Chris had to stand on the corpse and twist the handle to pull it free. It jerked out with a slurping suction.

Chest heaving, Chris looked down upon the ruined face of his betrayer.

The only sound was the ear-piercing, frantic scream of the fire alarms.

***

The gruesome reverie was interrupted by a sound from outside: through the cacophony of alarms, a sputtering engine, mewling and whining in its struggle to turn over.

Chris went to the front door.

Across the cobblestones, the Truck Driver

was in the dented, bullet-pocked, scratched-to-hell Ram, leaning over the wheel, cranking the ignition. The machine spat and sputtered and refused to spark to life.

A few dented cars remained. The paving stones were a mess of guts and blood scraped into tire tracks, dead dogs, dead old men, dead women, a few robed, most in various states of undress, some still masked or crowned, many crushed by fleeing tires, almost all maimed by Chris and the berserk dogs that had turned on them.

Chris marched across the porch and down the steps, then broke into a run.

***

The Driver saw him coming and reached for a pistol on the passenger seat. He swung it around to the driver side window but it was too late. Chris smashed through the glass with his ax.

He thrust through the hole, striking insanely, over and over. He struck the Truck Driver's left bicep, then his shoulder. The gun went off into the passenger side dash, setting off the airbag and knocking the pistol from the Driver's grip. Chris kept thrusting, stirring the blade around like a swizzle stick, tearing chunks from his adversary.

In his berserker rage, he gouged upholstery and flesh alike, smashed off the side mirror, and chopped the steering wheel to pieces. He dented and scratched the window frame and exterior. He partly scalped the Driver's huge head. He lopped the nose from the face.

The Truck Driver contorted and hollered.

A blow from Chris's weapon set off the driver side airbag. The Driver was bent toward the passenger side in a futile attempt to crawl out of reach. The deploying bag slammed into his side, crushing his elbow into his ribs. The big man shouted with confusion and pain.

Chris yanked the door handle. The open door chime rang out, soft and incessant: *Dingding-dingding...*

The burly Driver kicked out but Chris was already bringing down his ax in a wide semicircle. The heavy blade connected with a thigh, stripping a slab of flesh and taking off a whole cutlet. Purple blood fountained from the femoral artery. Body-hot fluid spattered against Chris's chest, neck, face, and spurted into his mouth.

Holding his right arm against his chest like a Boy Scout swearing allegiance to the flag, Chris threw his weapon aside, grabbed the Truck Driver by the legs with his good arm and yanked the man from the truck. It was a long drop. The Driver rag-dolled and hit the paving stones flat on his back.

Chris grabbed the burly man by his shirt collar and hauled him into a sitting position against the runner board of the big pickup. Then Chris walked to his weapon and lifted it from the earth.

Dingdingdingdingding...

He stood before the Truck Driver naked, caked in gore, the Driver's head level with Chris's blood-painted penis.

"You fuckin'," panted the Driver. "Fuckin' animal."

"MAN!" screamed Chris.

He swung the ax at the huge head, splitting the skull to the jaw. He heaved the blade free, raising it high.

"MAAAAANN!"

Chris struck the pulverized head, cracking the jaw and embedding the blade in the Truck Driver's thick neck. Again he raised the ax high and brought it down with blind fury. With every blow, he shouted "Man! Man! Man!" until the ax was unbearably heavy in his hand and his voice broke in a pubescent crack.

Through it all, the feeble alarm from the truck cried out like a helpless bystander, shrieking its electric horror.

Exhausted, Chris stumbled to the side and lost his grip on the heavy wood ax. It clattered to the stones.

The Truck Driver's head was a ruin. His neck and upper torso were split into great red sheaves like a rose blossom.

As the dawn bloomed, the smoky sky burned an otherworldly pink. Migrating ducks flew in v-formation above, their honks almost like the laughter of the Bobblehead.

Chris looked upon the truck driver the way he had once looked at two dead mallards in a pond. *Ding ding ding.*

A bit of movement under a car caught his attention. Someone hid there: a middle-aged, clean-cut man with close-cropped salt and pepper hair. He squeaked when his eyes met Chris's gaze. He scrambled further undercover like a salamander. But Chris was already bearing down on him at full tilt. The man bumped his head on the undercarriage. Chris was on him, dragging him out.

"No, no, no, no, no," the man begged.

Chris was silent.

The ducks passed away over the mountains.

On the porch, a shot pit bull still breathed, its little chest rising and falling with a slow,

208

steady rhythm.

Epilogue: Wieners At Last

Through the nocturnal quiet of the woods, Chris heard the crack of sparks and a murmur of human noise. He followed the sound until he saw the wavering yellow glow of flames. He found two men in canvas chairs mesmerized by the incandescent tongues of a bonfire.

He moved in silently, a log upraised in his hand. He brought it down on the base-ball-capped head nearest to him. The man further away jolted with surprise, cursed, and tipped over off his chair. Chris struck a second time. The log broke and the first man tumbled headlong into the fire.

The second man thrashed about in a panic, kicked the crumpled chair from himself, and scooched backward on his ass toward the shadows.

"Fuck!"

Chris's dead right arm swung like a flipper as he fell upon the second man. With his good fist, he pummeled the face until it was smashed beyond recognition.

They had wieners and Chris ate the whole pack raw.

About the Author

Gavin Ford was born and raised in Saskatchewan. He lives in Victoria, British Columbia.

About the Author

Gavin Torvik was born and raised in Saskatchewan. He lives in Victoria, British Columbia.

Other Books From

Scarlet Hosanna: Three Tales of Death Triumphant
by Henry Ben Edom

Where The Worm Never Dies
by Quinn Hernandez

Doomsday Daytrip
by Rob Ramirez

Cigarette Lemonade
by Connor de Bruler

Temperance Holocaust
by BJ Swann
and Elizabeth Bedlam

**FOR MORE BOOKS CHECK OUT
SWANNBEDLAM.COM**

FOLLOW US ON INSTAGRAM
@SWANN.BEDLAM

BECOME AN ARC READER EMAIL US AT
SWANNANDBEDLAM@GMAIL.COM

Printed in the USA
CPSIA information can be obtained
at www.ICGtesting.com
JSHW030817060524
62425JS00007B/15